A BREAK IN THE CIRCLE

© Devansh Kantha

Sharmila Kantha leads a peripatetic life as the wife of an Indian diplomat, while retaining her roots in Patna. Her previous publications include a novel, *Just the Facts, Madamji* (Indialog, 2002), a work of non-fiction, *Building India with Partnership: The Story of CII 1895-2005* (Penguin, 2006), and two picture books for children (Children's Book Trust). Currently based in Colombo, Sri Lanka with her husband and son, she is also consultant to a leading industry association.

A Break in the Circle

SHARMILA KANTHA

HarperCollins *Publishers* India
a joint venture with

New Delhi

First published in India in 2010 by
HarperCollins *Publishers* India
a joint venture with
The India Today Group

ISBN: 978-81-7223-931-2

2 4 6 8 10 9 7 5 3 1

Sharmila Kantha asserts the moral
right to be identified as the author of this work.

HarperCollins *Publishers*
A-53, Sector 57, NOIDA 201301, India
77-85 Fulham Palace Road, London W6 8JB, United Kingdom
Hazelton Lanes, 55 Avenue Road, Suite 2900, Toronto, Ontario M5R 3L2
and 1995 Markham Road, Scarborough, Ontario M1B 5M8, Canada
25 Ryde Road, Pymble, Sydney, NSW 2073, Australia
31 View Road, Glenfield, Auckland 10, New Zealand
10 East 53rd Street, New York NY 10022, USA

Typeset in 10.5/13.5 Meridien
InoSoft Systems

Printed and bound at
Thomson Press (India) Ltd.

For everyone in my extended family, with love
And especially for Devansh, Ashok and Ma

1

Tuesday

'GIRISH CHANDRA VERMA is coming to Patna after twenty years and he wants to stay with us. I received a letter from him this morning.'

Pranab tossed this weird announcement into the room and picked up the morning's edition of the *Times of India* and his reading glasses. Anuradha's mind buzzed with curiosity, but the wall of the newspaper was solidly between them now. She stopped pouring the tea and tried piercing the wall with her gaze.

'Which Girish Chandra Verma?' she asked, with a hint of exasperation.

Pranab lowered the newspaper and looked at her irritably over his reading glasses. 'I've told you about him,' he declared. 'He was my sociology professor in the university. Then he went off to some college in America and hasn't returned to Patna since.'

It was quite possible that during the eighteen years she had been married, the topic of Girish Chandra Verma had come up, but was she expected to remember every single conversation she had had with her husband over the years?

Anu resumed pouring the tea, still annoyed. But she knew further questions would only bounce off her husband at this time of day. She placed the cup on the table in front of him. It was a nice Hitkari cup, white with blue flowers and a slim gold edging. She had bought the tea set only recently and took quiet pleasure in the cup, as it sat, sparkling and elegant, on its matching saucer. It deserved admiration until the inevitable happened and the maid destroyed the set. The tea it held was the special Darjeeling leaf tea which Pranab enjoyed, delicately tinged with a drop of milk and liberally laced with sugar. Without looking up, he picked up the cup and sipped and Anu could hear a small sigh of satisfaction as he placed the cup back on its saucer. During the day, Pranab had to suffer the tea that came round in cheap glasses in a wire container carried by a cheerful but not-so-clean tea boy at the bank. At home, Anu shared the strong grain tea made by the part-time maid at mid-morning. This evening ritual of leaf tea in a proper Hitkari cup from a pot on a tray covered with a traycloth was an assertion of class.

Anu poured her own tea, then served Pranab the snack he relished every day on his return from the bank—chuda-matar, fried beaten rice accompanied by a sauté of peas, onions and tomatoes. It was so convenient to have frozen peas available in the market now. Earlier, this snack was limited to the winter months, and summer snacks, like onion pakodas or alu-poha, had to be tolerated until the first peas arrived. The time to really question Pranab about Girish Chandra Verma would be when he had finished his snack and tea and was changing into his pyjama-kurta. The rituals of daily life held precedence over unexpected visitors.

The warm tea slowly relaxed Anu. She realized they were getting low on tea already.

Did we have more visitors this month? Yes, Surendraji dropped in a few times during his morning walk. He tells his wife he is out walking, but he sits in people's houses, has tea and reads the newspaper. *Why would a person not visit his hometown for twenty years? That's longer than I have been married.* Twenty years ago, I was just completing my graduation. I didn't even know Pranab then, he had already finished college and joined the bank. His first posting was in Patna, perhaps he remained in touch with this professor then. *What will I talk to him about?*

Her thoughts were interrupted by her son rushing in from the field like a little tornado. Golu—no, Arnab, Anu hastily corrected herself—barged into the room, red-faced and sweaty as always, hair standing at all angles, flaunting various scratches and bruises; he flung his bat into the corner, jumped onto the sofa and gulped the glass of water that Anu had kept for him on the tray.

'I made fourteen runs today!' he grinned at his mother. 'Vikas tried to bowl me a very fast one. He came running from the end of the field, very fast, and threw the ball full speed. But I was ready, I had my bat in position like Sachin, and I hit it hard and it went right over Ravi's hands at the boundary and it was a S-I-X!' He lifted his hands up in the air in exuberance.

'Very good,' smiled Anu. She loved looking at her little boy when he came in from the field, excited about his day's achievements, relating them to her, his face still flushed and his hair on end. He would be ten in a couple of months, and was almost as tall as her already, but still, he was her little baby. Radhika was fourteen, serious and studious. She was in the bedroom finishing her homework. With Arnab, Anu knew she would have to struggle another half an hour or so before she could manage to get him to the study table. 'Now go and wash your hands and face.'

But Arnab had already switched on the TV and was piling his plate high with chuda-matar, his attention on the cartoons. 'Wash your face and hands!' Anu repeated sternly.

'In a minute,' Arnab mumbled, shovelling chuda-matar into his mouth.

'Go and do what your mother says,' said Pranab mildly from behind the newspaper, and Arnab put down his plate and rushed to the sink to wash his hands perfunctorily. Within seconds, he was back on the sofa and in front of the TV, wiping his hands hastily on his shorts.

Anu picked up the plates and the tea tray and carried them back to the kitchen. *For once, he should've done what I said. I must seem like such an ineffectual and helpless mother.* Asha didi certainly thought so, and Pranab always agreed with his sister. But Arnab was just a little boy, and didn't all boys listen only to their fathers? Asha didi always praised her own sons, like she never had any problems with them. *Are people really satisfied with their lives all the time?*

Dinner was ready to be served, but first there was the small matter of getting Arnab's homework done and the mystery of Girish Chandra Verma to be solved.

She broached the subject when they were sitting at the dinner table. Arnab's homework had taken longer than expected and the pyjama-kurta ritual was over by the time she emerged from the children's room.

'So tell me about this Girish Chandra Verma. Why is he coming here and why is he staying with us?' she asked after she had served the family potato-eggplant curry, okra and chapattis, and they were all busy eating except Arnab, who was preoccupied with a cockroach that had wandered onto the table. Anu flicked the cockroach off the plastic tablecloth and gave him a stern glance.

'Who is Girish Chandra Verma?' asked Arnab, his interest aroused immediately. 'Is he a friend of Papa's? Is he going to stay with us? *Here*? In this house?'

'No, he isn't my friend,' replied Pranab. 'He was my sociology professor in college, but he was very different from the other professors. He liked to spend time with his students even after college hours and encouraged us to visit him. We often had long discussions with him through the evenings, on all sorts of topics. He wasn't married, come to think of it, he probably wasn't much older than us to begin with. He must have been there throughout my MA, or had he left already...? No, I remember now. He left the summer after I completed my MA.'

Pranab paused to take another chapatti and some more curry.

'Where did he go? Why did he leave?' Arnab jumped in.

'There was an incident, I don't remember exactly what happened,' and Anu knew that the incident was still clear in his memory and was being censored for the sake of the children, 'but he had a disagreement with the head of the department, and after that it was difficult for him to stay on. He applied for some position in America, got the job and left. That was twenty years ago. I don't think he's visited Patna since. I heard he got married to an American girl and his family was not too happy.'

'So why is he coming back now?' asked Radhika, finally taking an interest in the story of this complete stranger.

'I got a letter from him this morning. It doesn't mention the purpose of his visit, but I know that his last surviving brother passed away recently. So maybe he needs to come back to settle his affairs.'

'Why is he staying with *us*? Why can't he stay with *his* family?' Arnab interrupted. It was so convenient to have curious children sometimes.

'He doesn't say in his letter,' Pranab said impatiently. 'It was only a short letter. It just said he would be staying with us. I didn't ask him why he couldn't stay with his family. And I won't ask him when he arrives either because it's rude to ask questions like that.'

'Did his letter say when he is arriving?' asked Anuradha, trying to placate him. *He thinks it's not his job to answer continuous questions from his children. He thinks that's the mother's job.*

'Yes, he will reach Delhi on the twenty-first and will take the one o'clock flight on the same day.'

It was already the thirteenth.

After dinner, it was time for the TV serials. Anu piled the dishes in the sink and on the kitchen floor, ready for the maid to wash when she came in the morning. Then she rushed to change into her nightgown before the serials began. As always, since she was the last to reach the drawing room, the sofa and armchair were already occupied and she had to haul a dining chair into the room.

But at least she was in time. In the first serial, the vile mother-in-law had just begun her machinations for the evening and the daughter-in-law was just awakening from her meek servile attitude, accompanied by great emotion and loud dramatic music.

In the next serial, an unmarried daughter was pregnant and there was confusion about the identity of the father. Who would marry her now! The man who had always loved her from a distance maintained that distance for the time being, but meaningful shots of his emotional face hinted that he may speak out for his beloved soon, perhaps in the next few months, after he had successfully overcome his mother's dominating presence. The girl's college friend, who had seduced her through vile deception, denied all knowledge. The rapist was still being sought by the police—and the possibility of the single diligent policeman falling in love with the girl was also suggested.

There was a half-hearted attempt to catch up with the news, but only Pranab was interested. It was bedtime for the children and Anu went to make sure they brushed their teeth and prepared their bags for school the next day. She hated running around looking for socks and pencils while preparing tiffin-boxes and getting the children ready in the morning.

Experience had taught her that if something unexpected awakened Pranab before his alarm rang, she would be subject to a few choice, though not ill-tempered, rebukes about being more efficient, being a better mother. And over the years, she had learnt that she need not always hear him out silently, she could also disagree sometimes.

When she switched off the light and got into bed, Pranab was still watching the news, but she remained awake until he came to the bedroom.

'This Girish Chandra Verma, why did he leave the college here?' she asked as soon as he got into bed.

'You know Manvi Prasad, the daughter of the IG Police Kamlesh Prasad? She was in my class. A very brash and aggressive girl. It was something to do with her. Apparently, she was friendly with him and her father didn't like it because he was only a lecturer and he wanted to get her married to an IAS or IPS. But personally, I felt he wasn't the type to get friendly with his female students. He had other preoccupations. He was too busy fighting the university establishment.' He paused for an instant, but Anu knew he had more to say. 'Girls can be so silly,' he said finally. 'Madhu once told me that girls chose sociology as a subject just so they could be in his class and moon over him. He was not particularly good-looking, but I suppose they were all stuck on him because he was young, single and such a passionate speaker.'

Anu suddenly remembered Anand. In college, she had cast soulful glances at him and even written poems about him! *I wonder why I was so taken with him then... He is such a pompous middle-aged bore now. We all need some romance in our lives.*

'The boys were not much better either,' Pranab continued. 'A lot of them found Manvi Prasad very attractive. I never liked her though. She was much too brazen for me. She used to take part in college plays and travel on college trips. This so-called romance between Girish sir and Manvi was the talk of the town at the time. Some said he actually left Patna because he wasn't allowed to marry her.'

As Pranab lapsed into silence, perhaps recalling his college days, Anu turned her back to him to indicate that she was ready for bed. He was lost in his past and she was glad he let her sleep.

Manvi Prasad. Yes, I remember meeting her on occasion. She might have been attractive when she was young. A deep but impossible love story between the anti-establishment professor and his vivacious student? He would have noticed her in the dim hallways and the classrooms; her laughter and her voice, her very difference from everybody else would have drawn him. They might have secretly held hands, gazed longingly at each other. And then to be found out one day! The ignominy, the scandal, the loss of reputation. No wonder he never came back.

2

Wednesday

THE NEXT MORNING, Anu despatched the children to their respective schools and watched Pranab leave for work in his red Maruti 800. They had bought the car just after Radhika was born. Anu's mother did not consider travelling on a scooter with a small baby a wise practice.

The maid was late yet again. Her hours were theoretically from ten in the morning till lunch time. According to the maid, this meant that she was free to come any time between ten and one-thirty. Constant exhortation from Anu, to whom punctuality was important, had been of no use.

Today's excuse was that she had to go to the hospital on account of feeling nauseous the past few days. Her coy expression told Anu that the maid was pregnant yet again.

'Are you crazy?' Anu scolded her. 'You already have six daughters!'

'Ka karein? What to do, Maiji,' came the response from behind a pile of dishes in the kitchen. 'He wants a son.'

Since there was no complaint in the maid's tone, Anu assumed she agreed fully with his desires.

'What if you have a daughter again?'

'Then we will have to try again.'

'How will you feed and marry off so many daughters? Besides, being pregnant so often is not good for your health.'

'God will take care of everything. I have already found a boy for my eldest daughter. He even went to school till class seven, and runs a rickshaw belonging to a seth. It's good money, but now he wants to buy his own rickshaw. My daughter is young and hard-working, an asset to any family. She is working in three houses with me and earning six hundred rupees already. Why should we have a problem when we have so many to work?'

'How old is she?'

'Humra pata naeekhay. Fifteen? Maybe sixteen? She was born the year there was a drought in north Bihar. The boy's family has already seen and approved her and the relatives are coming tomorrow evening for the engagement ceremony. We are getting five chickens from the village market. It's cheaper there.'

Anu gave up trying to sort out the maid's personal life. These people were just not worried about their future, as long as they could be happy in the present. They worked when they felt like it, spent what they earned, and felt no remorse when times were tough. She, on the other hand, had spent her whole life being responsible. Getting an education, then adjusting to marriage with a person she had never met before, then the children. And now...?

After the maid had handed her a cup of tea, Anu picked up her phone and called her mother. It was a daily ritual. Amma never called her as she didn't want to interrupt Anu in her household tasks. It was Anu's duty to call her mother when convenient. Amma, the long-married wife of a retired official, was free all day, as she so often informed Anu.

'Kya ho raha hai?' asked her mother.

'Nothing in particular. Chal raha hai,' replied Anu.

'Have you had breakfast?'

After she had described to her mother the castigation she had dealt the maid for being late, the vegetables she planned to buy later and other significant details of her day, Anu finally asked, 'Do you know Girish Chandra Verma?'

'Yes, of course. My bhabhi's cousin was his mami. Everyone calls him Giru. He left Patna a long time ago and settled in America. He married an American girl, they had a son, but they got divorced a few years later. His brother died about six months ago. Kyon, kya hua? Why are you suddenly asking about him?'

'Pranab received a letter from him yesterday. It seems he is coming to Patna after twenty years and he wants to stay with us.'

'Why should he want to stay with *you*? You don't even know him. Doesn't he have his own family to stay with?'

'That's what I said. Pranab was his student in college and knew him quite well. Even so, wanting to stay with us is rather strange.' She did not add to that. Her mother had an active imagination and was prone to delivering dire warnings on all that could go wrong with other people's lives. If matters turned out satisfactorily, she would say it was because she had forewarned others to take precautions. But if something did go wrong, she could take satisfaction in 'I told you so'.

And as expected, she declared, 'It isn't *nice* having a strange man come and stay with you. Na-na, theek nahin hai. You will be alone in the house with him!'

'Don't be silly, Amma. Pranab says he is a very decent man. Besides, I'm not an attractive young girl any more, I'm almost forty.'

'How does age matter? Men can do anything anytime. Tell Pranab he can't possibly stay with you. Log kya kahenge?'

'I don't think he will stay very long. After all, he has his family here. I suppose he just wants Pranab to pick him up from the airport, and drop him home later. That much he can ask his old student to do.'

'When is he coming?'

'The twenty-first.'

'But that's the day Nisha mausi's daughter is getting engaged. You have to go for that. What will you do about Giru then?'

'Maybe he will want to rest. He is coming directly from America via Delhi. He will probably be tired.'

'I suppose you can always bring him with you. What time are you planning to come for Rajeev Lochan Sinha's daughter's wedding this evening?'

'Oh no, I forgot about that. I haven't even given my sari to be ironed.'

'Are you wearing the chanderi I gave you for Holi? That will look nice.'

'But I just wore that for the chhatti of Asha didi's nanad's new baby. I'll have to get the old red South-silk ironed.'

'Don't be silly. How can you wear *South-silk* in this heat? Don't you have some other sari?'

Yes, she had, many others, all of which had been worn many times over the years and were as familiar to the ladies of the community as their own saris.

Anu said, 'I'll find something. It's really hot these days, isn't it?'

'Of course, what did you expect! It is almost the end of Baisakh. Don't be late this evening. You must reach before the baraatis arrive.'

'Oh, when are the baraatis ever on time! I don't think we can reach before eight. The traffic is horrible these days. And I will have to make Arnab finish his homework before we leave. What time are you planning to go?'

'You know your Papa; he likes to be on time. The card says 7 p.m. but we'll probably reach earlier because Rajeev Lochan Sinha worked with your father for a while and also, he is Brij phupha's nephew.'

'All right, I'll see you there. Right now, I have to call Pranab and remind him about this evening.'

'Okay then.'

'Okay.'

Amma's life was full of people, relatives, friends, acquaintances; they surrounded her all the time, and she revelled in their attention. Her obligations to them mattered a great deal to her.

Anu couldn't get through to Pranab on his cellphone. He was probably busy with a customer and had switched it off. She just hoped he remembered the wedding and returned home in time.

Right. Now what was to be done about the guest? Anu looked around her home. It was a two-bedroom flat on the third floor of Suraj chacha's bungalow. Suraj chacha and Pranab's father were childhood friends because their fathers had been posted together for years in Bhagalpur. The flat had just been vacated when Pranab was posted to Patna after three years in the Raxaul branch, and they had rented it. Suraj chacha was happy that the flat was going to a family friend with a respectable job. The last tenant, a businessman, had been difficult to dislodge and had left only after Suraj chacha's second son, who lived on the first floor and was a lawyer, threatened legal action. The threat was accompanied by regular severing of electricity and phone lines, and backed by his friendship with the police chief of Khagaria.

Sometimes it was useful to have relatives, friends and acquaintances in the city.

They had been here more than three years already and did not plan to move for at least another eight years by which time both Arnab and Radhika would have finished school. There were enough branches of the bank in Patna to keep Pranab in rotation for that long, taking into account the regional office and the special branch for industry.

Where is he going to stay in this flat?

It wasn't that they hadn't had guests before. Pranab's sisters Asha and Madhu often visited with their families, and various aunts, uncles and cousins were always dropping in to deal with medical problems, their children's college admissions, shopping for weddings and other matters that necessitated a visit to the city.

But none of them had lived in America for twenty years. Living in America meant that a person had become sophisticated. He would look down on having to share a room with a talkative ten-year-old, let alone making do by tossing a mattress on the drawing-room floor. And someone who had once been married to an American! He would be used to a very different lifestyle. Eating out of bone-china rather than melmoware. Or drinking Coke instead of water. Or using hot water from the tap for his shave. What if he needed *toilet paper*?

There were so many things to think of. Anu suddenly noticed that the embroidery on the cushion covers she had bought from an exhibition of Rajasthani handicrafts a year ago was fraying. There were empty spots where once there had been bright mirrorwork. The cushions themselves were sagging. The antimacassars on the sofa had been washed too many times and the fawn had become a dirty cream. The embroidery of the little girl with the big hat, replicated on the backrest and the arms of the sofa and the armchairs, was also in tatters. The plastic tablecover that protected the 'good' tablecloth on the dining table was stained with indelible remnants of haldi and other spills.

Well, this might actually be a good excuse to go shopping… The thought made Anu feel much better and she started preparing lunch, mentally making a list of things she could present to Pranab as being absolutely essential for hosting an America-returned guest. Toilet paper, she thought as she ground onions, garlic and ginger with cumin and coriander seeds. A plastic tablecover to replace the filthy one, as she sliced onions and threw them into the hot oil in the karahi. Cushion covers, maybe the appliqué type that Suraj chacha's oldest daughter-in-law did business in, stirring the ground spices into the fried onions. As she chopped the tomatoes, she thought of the number of women who were running businesses selling appliqué, 'designing' saris and cushion covers and bedcovers, making money out of the labours of poor women.

'Alu-lauki again!' protested Arnab when he returned from school and inspected the lunch prospects. 'Yuck!'

'Don't be so ungrateful about food, Golu,' Anu scolded him as she ladled out dal, rice and vegetables for him. He liked to eat rice at lunchtime, mixing it with the vegetables and dal into one big mush and gobbling it down. 'Did you get much homework today?'

'Well, I couldn't finish the maths classwork so I have to do that at home; and in Hindi, I have to do five question-answers from the end of the lesson and I don't remember what I have in science... some silly experiment with water.'

'We have to go for a wedding in the evening so you must hurry up and finish it all before we go.'

Arnab stopped eating and looked at his mother in dismay. 'Oh, no! What wedding! Whose wedding! How will I go, I have to do so much homework.'

'Do it before we leave.'

'I can't do that! I have to go for the match! I'm the *captain*!'

'Sorry, but you're not going out to play today.'

'Just for some silly wedding! I don't want to go.'

'Don't be ridiculous, you know we can't leave you behind alone.'

'Can't you drop me to Nani's house? I can do my homework there.'

'Nani is also going for the wedding.'

Arnab glowered at his plate. Then he thought of something. 'Will Debu also be at the wedding?'

'Probably,' replied Anu, quailing at the thought of a prolonged argument with her son. 'Vikas and Harsh might also come.'

Arnab resumed his lunch. Radhika huffed up the stairs, lugging her heavy schoolbag, and Anu went into the kitchen to make hot chapattis for her. At least, she wouldn't have to cook dinner this evening.

That was the only saving grace of the evening's function. After much thought, Anu pulled out her blue tissue from the nether recesses of her cupboard, thinking it fortuitous that the blouse of the new chanderi matched her old wedding sari. But then, the blouse for Radhika's Rajasthani lehenga had become too small for her and she refused to wear Anu's black blouse until Anu pinned up the chunni artistically to hide it. Arnab got most of his sums wrong while Anu was busy with Radhika and she had to do them all for him on a piece of paper for him to copy into his homework book. Thankfully, boys were not so conscious about clothes or Arnab would have protested about having to wear the black trousers which had been let out at the cuffs. Pranab went about his daily ritual of sipping tea, reading the paper, eating his chuda-matar and going to the bathroom, oblivious to his wife's frenzy. When he was ready, he shut all the windows and switched off the lights, even though Anu was still frantically draping her sari.

Finally, once the front door was securely fastened with the big brass Godrej lock, Anu dropped the keys into her purse and they all proceeded carefully down the dimly lit stairs and took their places in the decrepit red Maruti.

Pranab took Fraser Road, hoping it would be less

crowded, though whichever road one took in Patna invariably turned out to be the slowest one.

'How much cash have you put in the envelope?' asked Pranab as he braked to avoid a rickshaw-wala who had stuck out his right hand to indicate a right turn and then turned straight into Pranab's path, pedalling furiously and ringing his bell piercingly as if that would automatically make all other traffic vanish. 'Why is this fellow honking behind me? Do I look like I've stopped for a cigarette break?'

'I thought two hundred would be enough. What do you think?'

'Better make it four.' He put the car in gear and drove on sedately. 'There are four of us going... it should at least look respectable.'

Anu pulled out the bright red envelope with the gold Ganesh inscribed on it that she kept for such occasions and looked around in her purse for hundred-rupee notes. 'I don't have any new notes.'

Pranab stopped the car again, this time to let a couple of cows cross the road imperiously. 'What difference does it make? They'll just toss it onto the pile and write our names in the notebook, they're not going to see how new the note is. Golu, do you know the meaning of "Don't look a gift-horse in the mouth"?'

'The road is clear now, Papa,' Arnab pointed out, tactfully avoiding the question.

'It means one shouldn't find fault with gifts,' Radhika piped up, trying to show off.

They were waiting for the red light to change at the Dak Bangla crossing—or rather, for the policeman's signal, since the traffic signal wasn't working again—

when Anu remembered she had planned to ask Pranab about taking her shopping. It was the association of this crossing with J.G. Carr, the shop which sold foreign products like sausages from Ranchi, ancient cans of baked beans and outdated boxes of porridge, and cosmetics, creams and tissue paper, and other such useless items. The shop was now closed, and Ranchi's piggery had long been shut down, but childhood associations still lingered.

'Listen, I need to buy some things before this Girish Chandra Verma arrives.'

'Okay. When do you want to go?'

'Actually, I need to buy quite a lot of things. Could you drop me at Mira di's place on your way to the bank on Saturday? I will go with her to Hathua Market, and you can pick me up on your way home. We can drop the children at Amma's house.'

She knew that if she mentioned household items, Pranab would disagree with the need to purchase them. But he was not distracted by Anu's prevarication. 'What all do you have to buy? You won't get vegetables at Hathua Market.' The tangled lines of cars, rickshaws, cycles, carts and other assorted vehicles heaved ahead with a jangle of horns and bells. Pranab tried to force his way into the right-turn lane. 'And Saturday is too early for buying the vegetables anyway.'

'I haven't made the list yet but our old tablecloth is in tatters and maybe I should buy some new mats and sofa covers… little things like that.'

'But why are you going through all this trouble for Girish sir?' He resolutely ignored the honking behind him and finally inched his way into the right-turn lane.

By the time the lane moved forward, the policeman had his palm up, his whistle blowing a harsh long 'Stop!' Pranab switched off the engine. 'He's a homely person, it won't matter to him what the house is like.'

Anu waved to Shyama, a one time college-mate, who was in the car next to them. 'No, but I do need to replace the things that are in pretty bad shape, so I might as well do it before he comes. I will ask Amma to come with me, if you are busy.'

'I want to go shopping too,' Arnab announced from the back seat. 'I need a new pencil-box and Camel paints.'

'You always want something whenever Mummy goes to the market!' complained Radhika. 'Mummy, could you buy me some socks and school ribbons when you go?'

'Mummy, look how mean Didi is being! How come she can ask you to buy things and I can't?'

'Because I really need new socks and ribbons,' snapped Radhika. 'My school socks have holes and the ribbons are fraying. Your pencil-box is brand new compared to mine.'

'No, it's not.'

'Yes, it is.'

'No, it's not.'

The policeman whistled again and the mass of vehicles surged forward. Pranab made his right turn to the chorus of squabbling children, while Anu said hello, how are things, to Shyama when their cars drew alongside. 'Maybe you can ask him what he needs. That might tell us how long he is planning to stay,' he suggested. 'He sent his e-mail address—girishcverma at the rate yahoo dot com.'

'I don't know how to e-mail,' said Anu, trying not to sound sullen about Pranab's reluctance to spend money.

'I know!' piped up Arnab from the back seat. 'I can help you.'

'Good,' replied Pranab. 'You can show Mummy what an e-mail is. It's time she learnt anyway, and it will teach you to be responsible as well.'

The traffic spread out on the broad avenue and the car picked up speed. Anu hastily rolled up her window so that the wind would not ruffle her hair. Conversation halted as Pranab would not commit to the shopping expedition, Anu was irritated with his attitude, and the children lapsed into a morose silence. By the time they reached the wedding venue, a field in front of the host's house, it was much later than Anu's optimistic estimate of 8 o'clock, and cars were still arriving. It took Pranab a while to find a spot to park and he finally ended up with the back of his car sticking out onto the street due to a pipe lying on the verge.

The gate was decorated liberally with white tuberoses and red roses, and members of the girl's family were standing on the red carpet, waiting for the baraatis with heavy garlands in their hands. Anu and Pranab smiled and greeted the welcoming party, then made their way inside. Arnab had already joined the boys wearing embroidered kurtas and suits who wove their way between the legs of the elders, shouting and screaming as they ran. Radhika blended in with a group of young girls, dressed in heavily embroidered lehengas and glittering salwar suits, huddled together self-consciously. Inside the red shamiana, the women stood in twos and threes at one end while the men hovered at the other.

The elderly persons sat alone on the folding chairs and stared vacantly at everyone.

Anu saw her mother sitting with Nisha mausi near the shamiana entrance. Amma seemed to be bullying her younger sister who was looking more miserable than usual in the formidable presence of her overbearing sister.

'Namaste, Mausi, all going well for the engagement ceremony?' Anu greeted her cheerfully, bending to touch her feet.

Amma answered, 'Why shouldn't everything be going well for the engagement ceremony! I told Nishu to hire the halwai from Patna Market who cooked for Meena's wedding last year; he was very reasonable and his food is not too bad. So that is taken care of. As for the shopping, that we can do next week itself. But now she has a new problem.'

'What?'

'Nanni wants to enter some *modelling* competition!' Amma announced dramatically. 'It's out of the question, I told her. Log kya kahenge?'

Amma considered Nisha mausi to be the most wretched person in the family. First, she had not been able to acquire a husband befitting the standards of the family because she was dark-skinned. The family, unable to put together sufficient dowry to compensate for her skintone, had compromised and fixed her marriage with an unemployed graduate in the hope that his very respectable family would aid him monetarily. Nisha mausi had had to settle down with her new husband in the family home, where she had to deal with a vixen of a mother-in-law who constantly castigated her son's misfortune in getting such a dark-skinned wife. In due course, Nisha mausi's miseries were compounded by the birth of two daughters, both equally dusky. When, under the constant pressure of her mother-in-law, Nisha mausi had a third child, the inevitable happened and yet another girl was born, dark-skinned, of course. A dreary decade later, the mother-in-law was diagnosed with cancer and Nisha mausi was compelled to nurse her through the long illness until she passed away, ungrateful and unpleasant to the last. Her death left Nisha mausi in charge of the household—a retired father-in-law devoid of any sense of responsibility, a husband who was unable to keep any job for long and fast running out of options, three dark-skinned daughters, an elder sister-in-law who assumed the role of critic, various other inconsiderate sisters-in-law who kept turning up to stay for long periods, a brother-in-law who held a respectable job and whose wife therefore refused to help with the household tasks and, finally, another brother-in-law still studying.

The real tragedy came when the girls were in their teens. Nisha mausi's husband collapsed at his desk at work, was hauled to the hospital and promptly declared dead on arrival. The shock was enormous. Nisha mausi had to be kept sedated for three days. The father-in-law was reduced to a gibbering wreck. The daughters wailed constantly, except Nanni who was too young to comprehend the extent of the tragedy. Fortunately, the youngest brother-in-law, who had always respected his bhabhi, stepped in to take over the responsibility of the family. Having completed his studies, he had sat for the premier civil services exam and made it to the revenue services. Still single, he devoted himself to his family without hesitation. He was the one who pulled them through the tragedy, sending money regularly, looking them up at frequent intervals, and, above all, daring to admonish his elder sisters when they blamed the misfortune on the ill-fated bhabhi.

Things had stabilized since. The brother-in-law in Delhi, now married, had opened his doors to his nieces and they had amply returned the generosity by working hard and helping to look after their younger cousins. The eldest daughter had sat for the civil services exam under the able tutelage of her uncle and was now in the railway services. There had been no problem in finding her a suitable match and it was her engagement the following week. There was no demand for dowry, as lifelong free travel on trains was guaranteed for the immediate family and the prospective groom's family would be able to access rail tickets at short notice for themselves as well as for those persons on whom they wished to bestow favours. The second daughter was practically settled as she was in her first year of post-graduate studies in information technology. The youngest had joined Delhi University just last year.

And now she wanted to become a model!

'You should have *told* her not to take part in those college competitions, Nishu. Now the girl thinks she is as good as those silly models who keep winning the Miss World. She doesn't realize that it is all a conspiracy by Western cosmetic companies to trick our young girls into adopting their culture so they can sell more cosmetics.'

Anu said mildly, 'What modelling competition does she want to take part in?'

Again it was Amma who answered. 'What difference does it make... Oh no, here comes Mira. Don't mention anything about this to her, she'll spread it all around. It's best to keep quiet until we can persuade Nanni not to do it.' She fixed such a false smile on her face that anyone who knew her would know instantly that she was hiding something.

'Pranam, Lata bua. Pranam, Nisha bua.' Mira di came up and touched their feet.

'Khush raho, Mira,' greeted Amma, her smile intact. 'How are you? Did you find an English tutor for Debu?'

'Not yet, Bua. Hello, Anu. Where on earth did you dig up this old sari from?'

Amma replied, 'I told her to wear the new chanderi I gave her for Holi, but she insisted on taking out this ancient tissue sari.'

'Actually, I haven't been able to buy anything new recently,' Anu interrupted. 'Bank officers don't get as much "salary" as engineers.'

Amma dispensed with the smile to glare at her daughter, while Mira di, who was not astute enough to notice Anu's emphasis on salary, tittered triumphantly.

There was a sudden excitement at the gates as the drums and wailing shehnais became louder.

'Let's go, it looks like the baraatis have arrived,' said Mira di, her face shining as she headed towards the entrance.

'Why did you have to tell her your husband doesn't earn much!' hissed Amma. 'You always let your tongue run wild in company. I've been telling you to watch what you say since you were a little girl...'

'Don't you want to watch the arrival of the baraat?'

Anu replied. Hadn't she stopped talking altogether because of her mother's constant nagging?

'It'll take them another half hour to reach, they'll all be singing and dancing... oh, hello, Munni, what's happening?'

'Pranam, Chachi. Pranam, Nisha mausi. Hello Anu, all well?'

'Pranam, Munni didi. How are you?'

'Good. I heard Giru bhaiyya is coming to stay with you next week?'

'Yes, he sent Pranab a letter.'

'I wonder why he is coming back after all these years.'

'I have no idea, Munni didi, he didn't say anything in his letter.'

'You know about that scandal with his student Manvi and why he had to go away, don't you?'

'Anu was too young then,' said Amma. 'No one talked about it, it was all hushed up.'

'Then how does everyone know about it?' Anu said but they ignored her.

Munni didi went on. 'He was such a brilliant student. Everyone expected him to perform very well in the exam and make it to the civil services. But he hardly put in any effort. He was already teaching, but it was obvious that Manvi was the real distraction.'

'Giru failed in the exam, all because of her,' Amma took up the story. 'It was dreadful. Her father was so keen she marry a police officer like him, and if Giru had made it he might have been considered a suitable match. But Kamlesh wouldn't hear of her marrying a lecturer with no prospects. Manvi created a big hungama...'

'Apparently she even ran away from home in the middle of the night once and was found a few hours later in the neighbour's house by her frantic father,' continued Munni didi. 'He was furious.'

'I always say, let the children marry if they find their own partner,' pronounced Amma virtuously. 'Otherwise, later they will always blame the parents for everything.'

Arnab came running up. 'Pranam, Nani. Pranam, Nisha nani. Mummy, can I have some food now?'

'Shh, Golu, how can you have food when the baraat hasn't even arrived!' rebuked Amma. 'You'll have to wait until after the jaimaal is over and they have been taken to the food tables.'

'But I'm very hungry!' wailed Arnab. 'It's past ten already!'

Anu put a hand on his shoulder. 'Okay, let's go and see if there are any peanuts where Nana is sitting.' The conversation about the professor was abandoned.

There were no peanuts where Anu's father and his older brother sat silently, looking identical in loose trousers and half-sleeved shirts of indeterminate colour, large spectacles and white moustaches, canes propped up next to them. They looked up with matching grins when Anu and Arnab approached. After the pranams were over and blessings had been dispensed, Anu said, 'These weddings take so long. Poor Golu is starving.'

Chachaji leaned forward. 'Poor Golu! You are very hungry, aren't you?'

'Yes, Nana,' Arnab sighed. 'I haven't eaten for hours!'

Chachaji smiled in a conspiratorial manner. 'I know what to do about it. Come with me.'

He picked up his cane and hoisted himself painfully upright. Then the old man and the boy set off. Anu watched them disappear behind the cloth wall where the kitchen had been set up. The drumbeats of the approaching baraat indicated that the dancing on the streets was not yet over.

'So Giru is coming next week?' Papa asked as Anu sat down on the plastic chair next to him. It was good to sit after standing for so long. When the baraatis arrived, all the chairs would have to be given up to them.

'Yes. I don't know why he is staying with us though.'

'He doesn't like to talk about it, but his brothers had quarrelled among themselves for the village property belonging to his family. They were five brothers, Giru was the youngest, and after their father passed away they decided to divide the property, but they couldn't agree on the actual shares. The dispute continued for several years, and the land was farmed by workers who stole most of the produce. The brothers stopped talking to each other and finally the case went to court. Giru tried to resolve matters but couldn't. Now his brothers have died, so the next generation will fight over the land and the court case. He must be coming for that. Since the brothers weren't on talking terms, maybe he can't stay with his bhabhi.'

'What a terrible thing it is to have property!'

'It is not so much property that causes rifts within families. It is the ego that gets in the way. See that woman in the blue sari? That's Manvi.'

Anu knew Manvi, but they had barely exchanged more than a polite namaste. Daughters of senior police officers were an altogether different and exalted caste, not expected to mix with the rank and file. She looked at the other woman, flaunting her tall and still shapely figure, with a low-cut blouse and transparent chiffon sari draped low over her hips.

Such loud make-up and flamboyant gold jewellery! It drew attention to her face yet distracted from its ugliness. No middle-aged woman would wear such indecent clothes and overwhelming makeup in Patna. *I wonder what she was like twenty years ago, to have attracted the attention of a firebrand professor.*

Manvi looked at her just then; Anu smiled politely but Manvi did not deign to respond, preferring to pretend she was engrossed in conversation with the two men she was standing with.

'She is a lecturer in Arvind Mahila College,' Papa said. 'Her husband is in the police and gets transferred all over, but she doesn't go with him. It was very unsettling for the children, all these frequent transfers, so she stayed here with them. Of course, now they are grown-up and go to college in Delhi.'

A sudden quiet heralded the arrival, finally, of the baraat. 'Looks like the dwar-pooja has begun,' Anu commented. Although most people had moved forward to the gate to gape at the proceedings, despite having experienced many other such rituals, Anu and her father remained seated, content to wait until the procession swamped the space.

Someone turned up the volume of the stereo and the wailing of a shehnai filled the air. Golu and Chachaji returned from behind the curtain, Golu looking satisfied as only a ten-year-old with a stomach full of good food can.

'Nanaji took me to the kitchen,' he whispered to his mother, his eyes gleaming. 'I ate all the puris and alusabzi I could. Nanaji wouldn't let me eat the chicken though.'

'Whew, that's a relief!' Anu whispered back. 'Otherwise there wouldn't be any left for anyone else!'

Later, during dinner, Anu found herself standing next to Manvi Prasad, who now reluctantly acknowledged Anu's presence with half a nod. Anu smiled in return.

'Girish is coming to stay with Pranab next week,' Manvi stated without further preamble, as if Anu was unaware of the fact. 'It will be good to see how he is, what became of him after he left Patna.' She cast a sideways glance at Anu. 'You know, of course, that he was completely obsessed with me in those days.'

'Really?' answered Anu without revealing much interest.

'Yes, didn't you know? He left because I refused him!' She laughed, a tinny false sound. 'I was young and immature. I wanted something better.'

'Now he is a professor in America and you are a lecturer in Patna,' said Anu softly.

'And he is divorced!' She laughed the tinny laugh again. 'Maybe he still thinks of me. Tell him I would like to meet him. For old time's sake. Tell him that.'

'Okay.'

Manvi moved away after that, not keen to be seen any longer with Anu in her dowdy saree. Fuming at the lady's arrogance, Anu was distracted by Radhika complaining, 'There is nothing to eat, Mummy!' Anu persuaded her to take some rice and salad, but was sure the girl would not eat. *This obsession with weight is definitely another conspiracy by Western companies to trick our girls into adopting their culture!*

It seemed a long time before they were finally back in the car and heading home. Arnab dropped off to sleep almost immediately, and Radhika, after answering her mother's questions about the friends and cousins she had met, also fell silent. There was little traffic on the roads at this hour but Pranab's red Maruti was not conditioned for proceeding beyond a sedate forty, so they drifted down the dark avenues quietly, punctuated by desultory conversation between husband and wife.

'I saw Manvi there. She looked strange.'

'Yes, I told you that. She was like that in college also.'

'She wears so much make-up!'

'Does she? She talks too much.'

'Not to me, she doesn't. Does she talk to you?'

'No, I don't encourage her. But some people do.'

'Amma said Nanni wants to become a model.'

'A model! What gave her that idea? That's why I say girls should not go to Delhi. They come back with all sorts of ideas.'

'She is quite serious about it apparently. It's a good way to make money.'

'Don't be silly! She will never be able to get a respectable husband.'

'Munni didi was asking why Girish Chandra Verma is coming back.'

'Quite a few people mentioned it to me too. I was quite surprised; I don't think I told anyone except you.'

'I only told Amma. Maybe he wrote to other people also. Anyway, can I go shopping tomorrow?' Anu asked.

'Okay. You can come with me tomorrow morning and I'll withdraw some money for you. Then you can go with Mira di.'

'No, I think I will go by myself. It'll be quicker, and I can be back before the children come home.'

They had drifted into this habit of verbal callisthenics without realizing it.

'Mira di is always shopping,' Pranab remarked. 'I wonder how her husband can afford it.'

'She knows all the best shops,' Anu replied, avoiding the question. It would not do to run down her own family members in front of her husband. He would lose all respect for her if she admitted that there were people on her side of the family who were not exactly models of rectitude. Besides, she couldn't be sure that Mira di's husband was on the take, could she? 'I always ask her if I need to buy anything for the children, she knows where the best sales are.'

Mira di also had another problem not discussed except in hushed tones among ladies at family gatherings when the men were in another room. Her daughter was widely suspected to be a lesbian. She had had the same roommate throughout college in Calcutta and the two had continued to live together when they started working there after graduation. Then they both decided to do a management degree from a vague college in the south which no one had heard of, and they were still living together. Not only that, the daughter had refused all prospective grooms on the grounds that she first had to get settled in life.

During her infrequent visits to Patna, ladies at various times and in various groups had tried to explain to her that a career and marriage were no longer mutually exclusive options. Why, look at Sudha, she had not only completed her graduation after marriage but even finished her master's degree while carrying and caring for a baby, and with such distinction that she got a job with *Hindustan Times* and could now leave the children to her mother-in-law's care. Sudha had been rather young and still only in the first year of college, but that had been no reason to let a good match pass.

By now, Mira di's daughter was rather aged, nearing thirty, and the ladies of the community had just about given up hope of a good match for her. Even then, not much damage would have been done to the girl's reputation if two Hindi films had not opened the eyes of the Patna matrons. It was while clandestinely viewing these films in the confines of their drawing rooms when the husbands and children were out of the house that the truth about lesbianism had dawned on them. They could hardly be blamed for watching these movies, which were scarcely less than pornography with their almost explicit hinting at physical relationships between women, for, after all, the movies had won awards at foreign film festivals, hadn't they?

So Mira di had become the recipient of dismayed whispers about what her daughter was doing in the south and shouldn't she be forcefully married off now, or at least, weaned away from the terrible influence of that awful Bengali girl. It wasn't healthy, she was told, to be so close to the same girl for so many years. Mira di, if whispers were to be believed, had once even had a blazing row with her daughter about her companion, during which the daughter had proclaimed that she couldn't care less about what people were saying and that she would do as she pleased and live with whom she wanted, whether male or female. The next day, she had departed from Patna, ostensibly because term was starting in the college in the south. Her aunt, who had apparently been right in the next room, insisted that the row had not been serious and that the daughter had promised to get married to a person of her mother's choice as soon as she had landed a proper job, which would be soon since the management course was almost completed. But no one actually believed her because Mira di had not requested anyone to look for a suitable boy yet.

3

Thursday

THE DAY BEGAN chaotically. Arnab, never an early riser even at the best of times, didn't respond to Anu's vigorous shaking and muted pleas. She was finally reduced to actually dragging him out of bed, praying the noise wouldn't attract her husband's attention and send him rushing into the room. Radhika seemed to have gone off to sleep in the toilet and it took a lot of banging on the door to get her to come out. Following this was the ultimate tiffin problem. After being offered various choices by their doting mother, Arnab decided on Maggi 'two minute' noodles, and Radhika, who had to be persuaded every day to take tiffin at all, agreed on a jam sandwich 'with no butter'.

Anu rushed into the kitchen, put the water on to boil for the noodles, slapped the karahi on the other burner, prepared the jam sandwich and wrapped it in the bread paper, cut up potatoes for Pranab's lunch, tossed them into the karahi with a touch of panchphoran and garlic, added the noodles to the water, kneaded the dough, slid the noodles into the tiffin-box, put the griddle on the vacated burner, rolled out the parathas, stirred the potatoes, fried the parathas, and finally stuffed everything into Pranab's three-container hotcase. She cut up tomatoes and onions to fill the third container because, after all, he had to have healthy stuff as well.

The kids clattered down the stairs to their respective bus stops and Anu manned her post at the balcony to make sure that the rickety old buses did pick them up. She had a lot of work to get through before she could leave for the much-anticipated shopping expedition.

She had bathed, draped herself with the starched organdie sari with the appliqué work that she had bought the previous Holi and was combing her hair when the doorbell rang. She wondered who it was; she had already telephoned Anita downstairs to tell the maid not to come till two.

Comb in hand, she opened the door.

Kallu chacha filled the doorway, accompanied by his wife, his youngest daughter, a suitcase wrapped in blue camouflage cloth and an assortment of neatly packed plastic baskets.

Anu bent to touch their feet, barely managing to conceal her annoyance.

'Train-va doo-doo ghanta late aeel!' Kallu chacha burst out. 'It stopped outside Patna and just wouldn't move. I don't know why they can't stick to the schedule, especially when it leaves on time. Ae-ho, sunat-aru,' his usual mode of addressing his wife, 'take my shaving things out. And my trousers and shirt. Pinky, get me some water. And put some water to boil for my shave. No, I won't have any tea right now. I don't take anything until I have had my bath.'

Anu helped Chachiji lug the suitcase into the children's room while Pinky went into the kitchen to get the water. Kallu chacha continued talking, although no one was in the room. He preferred to use his native Bhojpuri with Anu. According to him, if a daughter-in-law entered a Bhojpuri-speaking household, it was incumbent on her to learn the dialect, and he continued to disapprove of Anu's use of Hindi while conversing with him, which implied that she would, alas, never be fully integrated into the family.

'So hot here already. Ranchi is much better. Where is Nabbu? Oh, is he in the toilet? Hum kahat raheen, I wouldn't come to Patna from April to October if I wasn't compelled to! But ka karein, I have to run up and down the whole state for Pinky's marriage, whatever the weather.' He gulped down the water Anu brought him in a steel glass, as well as the other glass meant for Chachiji.

'It is a good proposal this time. I met the boy's mama in Ranchi; he is an engineer, and the father is a lecturer in Muzaffarpur. He is coming to Patna for Nisha's daughter's engagement; he is from the groom's side. The boy can see Pinky and the whole thing can be decided here itself. The boy is a doctor at Arrah, his mother is from there, and his mama told me that he was doing very well. If it works out then I can retire in Ranchi in peace and play with my grandchildren. Hey bhagwan, betiyan ke biyah khatir ka-ka karey ke padey-la!' He took the plastic mug with the hot water that his daughter—apparently sufficiently inured to such sentiments from her father not to feel guilty about her existence—brought for him, the shaving equipment his wife was holding up patiently and plodded into the second bathroom.

Chachiji had already settled her suitcase and assorted plastic baskets in the children's bedroom. Now she said in failing tones, 'The journey was too long and I am exhausted. Ae, Pinky, tani chai lava-ho. I don't understand how Chachaji can get up and go out immediately. But .men have so much more energy than us women, they don't have to bear children. Pinky, go and help Bhabhiji make breakfast.'

She arranged herself comfortably on the sofa as only a matron with two grown daughters could. The other daughter was already married, and it was a given that following the marriage of the younger daughter, the only son would also be provided with a wife which would ensure the continued comfort of the matron, although the care lavished by a daughter could never be compensated with that of a daughter-in-law, but ka karee, a daughter was wealth that belonged to another and had to eventually go to her own home.

In the kitchen, Pinky looked at Anu's sari and asked, 'Are you going somewhere, Bhabhiji?'

'I was planning to leave with your bhaiyya and go to the market,' replied Anu, taking out some vegetables from the fridge.

'Oh, to the market! That's okay then. Why don't you go and change out of this nice sari while I cut the vegetables.'

Anu stormed into her room. Pranab was wearing a towel and combing his hair. He watched as she yanked off her sari. 'Don't tear up your sari just because you can't go to the market today. I'll take you another time.'

'How can I go at all!' Anu hissed. 'They are here until the engagement. There's a whole week left! Why did they come so early?'

'You know he likes to come to Patna frequently, even if he has no excuse. He has so many friends here.'

'He should stay with them then!'

'Don't worry, he will be out all day, and one of these days we'll tell him you have some urgent work in the market and you can go.'

Well, I have put in my mandatory protest and that's as much as I can do, Anu thought gloomily. *There is no way I can do up the house now before the arrival of the man from America. What difference does it make anyway? If he wants toilet paper, he can go and buy his own!*

Kallu chacha spoke continuously to his audience of admiring females while he had his breakfast, while he strapped on his well-worn sandals and even when he was halfway down the stairs. He had the important self-assigned task of making contact with as many members of the boy's family as were present in Patna. This major project was going to keep him happily occupied until the boy's father arrived. Then he would have to lobby him for a date on which the boy could view the girl.

It was then Chachiji's turn to proceed to the bathroom. She would spend the rest of the morning in her bath, pooja and breakfast, and with some television and gossip go on comfortably up to lunchtime. Thereafter, she could legitimately spread herself on Radhika's bed for a well-justified afternoon nap.

Pinky busied herself with cutting vegetables, this time for lunch, while Anu called Anita to tell her that her plans had changed, she could not go out, and could Anita send the maid at the usual time. Anita, exhibiting the natural curiosity of a neighbour, asked what had happened, was everything okay, and Anu replied in a voice slightly louder than usual that everything was fine, it was just that Kallu chacha and his family had arrived *very unexpectedly* from Ranchi in the morning and therefore she wouldn't be able to go shopping. But she wasn't sure if Chachiji heard her side of the conversation, as there was not the slightest flicker of contrition on her face. Then she went into the kitchen to prepare lunch.

When the phone rang, Anu knew it would be Amma and she was not disappointed.

'Why haven't you called, it's almost lunchtime. I've been waiting all morning for you to call. I'm coming today so we can discuss what to do about Nanni. Papa has to go to the club and he will drop me to your house in the evening.'

'Not today, Amma,' Anu said.

'Kyon, kya hua? Nanni is arriving tomorrow morning by Deluxe—her first-year exams are over—so we have to think about it today!'

'Kallu chacha and Chachiji are here with Pinky. They have to meet someone for Pinky's marriage.'

'Kallu is here again! Didn't he come and stay with you just two months ago?'

'Yes.' She refrained from pointing out that it was actually six months, since Chachiji was standing by, taking close interest in the conversation.

'Doesn't he have anything better to do than trouble you every few months? Sponging off you and making you cook his four meals a day.'

'Yes.'

'You should cook khichri for him every day. Tell him you have to spend all your money on your children's education.'

'Yes.'

'Anyway, I am coming this evening. You know how upset Papa gets if things don't go the way he's planned.'

'Okay.'

'Okay.' Amma hung up.

'Was that your mother?' Chachiji asked curiously. 'How is she? Is her arthritis better these days?'

Anu didn't bother to respond to the solicitous question, obviously rhetorical.

Can't I have privacy to talk to my mother without people breathing down my neck? As for Amma's suggestion to make khichri every day...

The rest of the afternoon was spent in mundane housework, including arguing with the maid who was not too happy to be faced with the additional utensils of three extra people, but in the interests of retaining her job couldn't protest much. Instead, she banged around the pots and pans, broke a cup and did a perfunctory job of the sweeping. Anu followed the maid around the house and chastised her for the bad sweeping. Chachiji was too engrossed in the re-run of last night's serials to notice her young relative's demonstrations of good housewifeliness. Finally, Anu plonked herself on an armchair and caught up with the serials she had missed on account of the wedding.

The policeman, who was attracted to the raped girl because of her courage, diligently continued his investigation by appearing for the umpteenth time at the doorstep of the rapist whose alibi had been confirmed by his sister-in-law who was in love with him. The policeman was close to confronting the sister-in-law, having finally figured out what the audience had known all along—that the sister-in-law believed that the rapist reciprocated her love and was therefore willing to substantiate his story. Sometime over the next few days, Anu expected the policeman would disabuse her of this notion and, in what was sure to be a dramatic episode, expose her feelings and haul the rapist away in handcuffs.

The children were quite happy to see Chachiji and Pinky. For them, it was a break from their usual routine and they spent the afternoon enthusiastically playing cards with Pinky in the living room, while Chachiji retired to the children's room for her afternoon nap and Anu isolated herself in her room to brood over inconsiderate in-laws and hope that her mother would not disgrace her by suggesting in their presence that she cook only khichri.

She was woken up by Arnab shaking her. 'Mummy, don't you want to send that e-mail? I have to go out to play soon. Come quickly, I have switched on the computer.'

Still a little disoriented, Anu pulled up a chair next to her son who was clicking away with the mouse, moving it at a dazzling speed across the pad. Finally, he stopped the frenetic clicking, pecked at the keyboard and told her to type out her letter, hold the mouse over 'Send' and click. Before Anu could even open her mouth, he was out of his chair and through the door.

'Don't forget to shut off the computer, Mummy,' he shouted as he raced down the stairs.

Anu stared at the keyboard. The words formed slowly in her mind and she tapped them out, letter by letter.

Dear Sir,

My husband informs me that you will be visiting us from next Tuesday. We will be delighted to have you. Please advise me about your particular requirements so that I may make the necessary arrangemements.

With kind regards,
Anuradha

She clicked 'Send', and then tried to figure out how to switch off the machine. After a while, as she was still examining it, the screen went blank.

Maybe the thing has auto shut-off, like the oven.

When Arnab returned from the field an hour later, he scolded her. 'Mummy, you didn't even disconnect! Papa will be very angry when he sees the bill. Oh look, there's a new mail.'

He flopped into the chair and clicked away rapidly. 'It's from the professor. Here, read it.'

Anu peered disbelievingly at the computer.

Dear Anuradha,

Good to hear from you! Thanks for your interest, but I fear I may have too many requirements for you to meet. So, as my students put it—chill!

Looking forward to being in Patna and meeting you both.

Best,
Girish

No mention of toilet paper and running hot water? And what exactly was 'chill'? Or 'best'?

'That was quick,' said Anu to Arnab. 'I thought it would take a day or so to reach.'

'Don't be silly, Mummy. It reaches as soon as you send it. Do you want to write another one?' He clicked and brought up the 'Reply' window.

But this time Anu was not sure what to write. As Arnab eyed her expectantly, she typed out an uncertain message.

Dear Sir,

Since you are coming here after so many years, I would like to inform you that we do not have running hot water in the house. Moreover, the quality of toilet paper available here is very doubtful. I hope you will not mind sleeping on a cot in the drawing room as my uncle-in-law and his family are also visiting. Maybe they will have left by the time of your arrival.

My husband is looking forward to your stay.

With kind regards,
Anuradha

Arnab told her to wait for a while in case there was a reply. She gazed hopefully at the screen, and in a moment, the message icon appeared.

Dear Anuradha,

It sure has been a long time since I was in Patna. But obviously, there has been a lot of progress. I didn't know that toilet paper of any quality was available there!

I think having me over will inconvenience you. On the other hand, it will be interesting to sleep on a cot in the drawing room. In the old days, we used to toss a mattress on the floor if we had extra guests, so this will certainly be a step up! For various reasons, I haven't been able to visit India in many years. So we still have not achieved running hot water, is it?

I would love to meet your uncle-in-law and his family. But I have to warn you that I do snore sometimes. So your uncle-in-law may not be so happy to meet me. :)

What else has changed in Patna in the last twenty years? Does the amaltash still spread its glowing yellow stain on the spring sky? Does the rain still sweep the town, pounding through the alleys during monsoon? Do people still drop in on each other for leisurely cups of tea? Do offices still open at 10.30 and shut down at 3?

I do look forward to catching up.

Gtg.

Cheers
Girish

Anu did not know what to think of the mail. Was he joking or was he serious? Maybe people who had been away from their homes and families for a long time became disconnected from their past. Maybe the invisible strands of relationships and commitments weakened and then faded away if people lived alone. That was why he sounded unlike anyone she knew. Anu wondered what living in isolation would feel like, with the freedom to do what she liked, whether to read or paint or go shopping. How long could one be alone and not worry about obligations, she wondered.

Dear Sir,

I hope you will not be too disappointed with our house. Everybody here remembers you well, and also the reasons you left Patna. So you will have no problem catching up with your relatives and friends. We went to a wedding last night, and many people spoke about your visit, although I don't know how they knew about it as neither I nor Pranab told anyone. It is strange how news travels so rapidly here.

To your questions about Patna, I have to answer yes. Why would these things, or anything, have changed?

We are all eagerly anticipating your visit.

With kind regards,
Anuradha

Anu checked that her spellings, grammar and punctuation were correct. After all, she was writing to an American professor. She clicked on 'Send' and waited for the response.

'But he's no longer there, Mummy,' Arnab informed her eventually.

Anu was surprised. 'How do you know? Can you see him over there in America?'

'No, Mummy! See here, he says "gtg", that means he has "got to go", and he's gone.' To avoid getting to his homework, he sat for a while longer, peering hopefully at the computer. But the message icon did not reappear, so he switched off the computer and took out his books.

When her mother arrived in the evening, just before Pranab reached home at 6.15, Anu expected her to begin with the virtues of khichri. But she was on her best behaviour, fully conscious of the obligations of a mother towards her daughter's in-laws. She had brought with her two kilos of mangoes and a kilo of besan laddoos.

'Namaste, Samdhinji,' she greeted Chachiji with complete deference. Chachiji was seated in front of the

TV again, but there was nothing interesting to watch, so she switched it off enthusiastically and returned Amma's greeting.

'Oh, namaste, namaste, Samdhinji. How nice to see you! How have you been? We came from Ranchi this morning. It was very pleasant there. Khoob achchhi hawa chalat rahey.'

Although both Amma and Chachiji were Bhojpuri speakers, Amma always spoke to Chachiji in formal Hindi, a rather more polite language than its genial offshoot, which could at times verge on the raunchy.

'Yes, it is very hot here. The loo has already begun and it is very unpleasant to go out during the day. Where is Samdhiji? Surely he has not gone out in this weather.'

'Ah, Samdhinji,' Chachiji sighed dramatically. 'Betiyan ke biyah khatir ka-ka karey ke padey-la! He has gone out to meet the boy's relatives. You know, we are looking for a boy for Pinky...'

And then she related all over again the present prospect, how they had got to know of the boy, which relatives Chachaji had already lobbied and what their future plans were. At this, Amma related with relish how families had lined up for Nisha's daughter 'who is in the railway service, as you may be knowing', and how clever the girl was and how handsome the boy was, 'absolutely milky-white complexion', and so on.

Meanwhile, Anu went about her evening duties diligently, preparing the chuda-matar, going over Radhika's homework, getting dinner ready with Pinky's help, all the while waiting for Amma to make an excuse and join her in the privacy of her bedroom so they could discuss the emergent disaster of Nanni's life. Eventually, when Pranab emerged from the bedroom, ready to take over the TV, Amma signalled to Anu by wiggling her eyebrows at her conspicuously.

Taking her cue, Anu said, 'Amma, could you please come into my room for a moment? I want to show you the sari I am giving Gunni for the engagement.'

Amma stood up at once. 'Where did you buy it from?' she asked and followed Anu towards her bedroom, abandoning Chachiji.

'From that shop on Boring Road where you bought my chanderi for Holi,' and talking thus, they escaped into the sanctity of Anu's room.

'She is coming tomorrow morning,' hissed Amma as soon as the door was closed.

'But what do you think you can do, Amma? If she wants to become a model, I don't see anything wrong with that.'

'Are you crazy? Do girls from respectable families go around displaying their bodies to anyone who wants to ogle! Log kya kahenge? We have to stop her at once, before she goes any further and we become the talk of the town.'

'Okay, okay. But how will you stop her?'

'You must speak to her. She won't listen to us; she thinks we are old and unreasonable. But she will listen to you. You are from the same generation and she has always looked up to you.'

'Nonsense. I am twenty years older than her. Why should she listen to me?'

'Don't you remember, when she was eight years old, and her father passed away, it was to you she kept coming for comfort.'

'That was because she wanted to play with Radhika.'

'No, no, it was because she really liked you. So you must speak to her. Tell her what a wrong line of work it is, tell her that she will soon become too old to remain a model... and what will she do then, without a career, without her looks, and without any prospect of finding a respectable husband. Tell her she cannot sell her body like a you-know-what. The family will not accept it. Log kya kahenge? So when will you meet her?'

'It is difficult for me to go out right now, Amma. I have people at home.'

'That doesn't mean you can't go out! After all, you have other things to do; you can't be expected to sit at home and cook for them all day. I'll ask Papa to take us tomorrow morning. You can tell Kallu that you have to help with the shopping for the engagement.'

'All right, then. I will be ready in the morning by eleven.'

'Good, so that's settled then.' Amma smiled triumphantly.

By the time they came out of the room, Kallu chacha had arrived and was busy gulping down the tea that Pinky had poured him. With him was a young man, probably in his mid-thirties. He was introduced as Gautam, Chachiji's nephew through various in-laws and cousins. He was visiting from Delhi, where he worked for a big multinational company. Kallu chacha viewed these companies with suspicion, having heard rumours that they tended to toss employees into the street whenever they felt like it, although they did pay well. But Gautam, tall and self-assured, didn't look like he was in constant fear of losing his job.

'Aha, aha, Samdhinji, how nice to see you here!' Kallu chacha greeted Amma. 'Sab theek ba, noo? I met your brother today, the one who lives in Kadam Kuan, he had come to my friend Rajesh's house, and we had lunch together. And how is Samdhiji? He didn't come with you? You know Gautam, of course, he is Bikramji's son. He is working in Delhi for... what's the name? I keep forgetting. You private sector people change your jobs so often!'

Gautam smiled and touched Amma's feet. He did not bother answering Kallu chacha's question and went to talk to Pranab instead.

'Samdhiji is fine. He dropped me off here before going to his club. He likes to play bridge there with his friends sometimes,' Amma replied; her words seemed to carry barbed messages to this interloper who was giving her daughter grief with his insensitive presence. 'He has been playing since he was in service,' *and has better things to do than visit Kallu chacha.*

'Good, good.' Kallu chacha happily picked up the gauntlet. 'He keeps himself occupied even in retirement.' *Well, he has no other constructive way to use his time, unlike me.* 'That's what I always say—you must have a hobby so that you don't get bored when you retire. I myself am so busy with Pinky's marriage. Ka-ka karey ke padey la betiyan ke biyah khatir! Where do I have the time to indulge in any hobby?'

'By god's grace, we were lucky to find good matches for our daughters quite easily.' *Whereas poor Kallu chacha was not similarly blessed. Further,* 'Pranab is such a wonderful son-in-law; he respects us as though we were his own parents.'

Kallu chacha couldn't let that pass. 'Yes, yes, all the boys in our family are very well brought up.' *Unlike the uncouth boys of your family, especially your brother-in-law's son, who disappeared years ago, leaving behind his wife and children. Never mind,* 'Your daughter is also so adjusting, she has fitted in so well,' *with my tolerant and kind family.*

'All my three daughters have fitted in very well with their families. Anu! Will you bring some of those mangoes for Samdhiji? I got them especially for him. It can't be easy to get such delicious mangoes in a small town like Ranchi.'

'Oh, no! Nowadays we get everything in Ranchi. Since it became the capital of Jharkhand, it's become a very important city. We see so many Ambassador cars with red lights flashing, moving around the city all the time. Laal batti jalaat ba, chalat-phirat ba. Looks like you haven't been there for some time, Samdhinji. There are so many modern markets and housing complexes now; you must come and visit us sometime.'

Anu smiled inwardly at this tug-of-war between Amma and Chachaji, both dominant and arrogant personalities. It got worse when she brought out the mangoes. Amma offered Kallu chacha the plate and the mangoes as if she was the hostess, whereas for Kallu chacha, this was his nephew's house, which made him the host. The 'pehle aap, pehle aap' ritual continued until Anu herself handed the plates and the mangoes to both parties, carefully making sure that she offered them first to her mother, who was indeed, technically, the guest.

Gautam lowered his lanky frame on to the sofa, next

to Amma. 'I am so happy to meet you. My mother used to talk about you often.'

Amma visibly grew in stature. 'Haan-haan, your parents and we were posted together in Danapur, long ago, when they were just married. It was just for a few months.'

Gautam turned to Anu. 'My mother told me that your mother taught her how to cook.' Anu couldn't help raising a sceptical eyebrow at such blatant flattery. Gautam responded with a bland smile.

Then he helped himself to the mangoes and pronounced them excellent, rapidly rising in Amma's esteem. 'In Delhi, what passes for langda mango tastes more like papaya. I wish I had been able to come here later in the year when the malda will be available.' He added, rather wickedly Anu thought, 'Of course, in Ranchi, it must be difficult to get good malda. Buaji must have to come all the way to Patna to get the true taste of the real mango.'

This led to another heated conversation about mangoes and the varieties available not just in Patna and Ranchi, but all over the country, and which was better for what reasons. Gautam smiled at Anu in what could only be described as a conspiratorial manner and left soon after.

Kallu chacha, never one to resist the opportunity for discourse, compounded matters further by inviting Amma and Papa to stay for dinner, adding that he knew parents didn't really like to eat in their daughters' houses, but surely Amma could not be so outmoded. Amma protested feebly, but realized that to disprove his contention she would have to stay, though she knew

Anu had already prepared dinner and would have to cook extra for her parents.

And so, Kallu chacha was assured of a suitable audience for the evening and he spent the time fruitfully by explaining in great detail his visits of the day and how they were bound to have a positive effect on Pinky's prospects.

Fortunately, it was soon time for the serials and chairs were brought in from the dining room to accommodate everyone around the TV.

The first serial showed Ramesh bhaiyya striding into the house from which his married sister was being thrown out. The sister clutched his feet and wailed that she didn't want to leave the house, it was her home and this was her family now. So what if they wanted to throw her out, a woman entered her husband's house in a doli and left only on an arthi. She implored him to explain this to her in-laws who were trying to throw her out; she wouldn't, she couldn't leave, she sobbed. The audience wept along with her, astounded by her inexplicable fidelity to her in-laws.

Amma and Papa decided to leave during the commercial break, Papa saying it would be unsafe to drive too late at night, given the number of car-jackings that had taken place recently. Amma regretfully agreed, insisting that she would catch up with the story the next day. Hurried goodbyes were said as the commercial break was almost over.

On her way out Amma, determined to have the last word, annonunced, 'Do you remember Giru?'

'Giru? No, I don't know him,' replied Kallu chacha unsuspectingly.

'Of course, you do; Akhilesh Chandra Verma's younger brother, who was a lecturer here,' Amma reminded him gently.

'Arrey haan—Girish! He was the one who got into that mess at the university with Manvi Prasad and had to leave town in disgrace. I believe he went to America, married some American girl and got divorced afterwards. Why are you asking about him suddenly? He has not been back in Patna since then.'

Triumphantly, Amma replied, 'He is coming to Patna next week. He will be staying here, with Anu.'

At long last, Kallu chacha was reduced to speechlessness. He gaped at Amma, but before he could recover, Amma had said namaste and swept out of the door, her head held high.

Anu went to see her parents to the car, and told them to call when they reached home. Amma exhorted her to be on time the next morning for the visit to Nanni. By the time Anu returned, the next serial about the unmarried pregnant girl was on.

The distant admirer of the pregnant girl was discussing his unhappy situation with an old female friend from college. Inevitably, this girl was in love with the admirer, and had been since their college days as she had confessed many episodes ago to another friend. Close-up shots of her anguished face were shown as the man she loved told her of his love for another. As he asked her for advice, running tortured fingers through his hair, 'Main kya karoon, Arunima, main kya karoon?' she cast down her heavily mascaraed eyes to mask her deep emotion. When she looked up, her eyes were glistening. It was a moving moment, so moving that it had to be alleviated with a commercial break.

After the break, the moment was repeated and to emphasize the emotion, in case the audience did not sufficiently appreciate her terrible dilemma, the glistening eyes were raised two more times in slow motion to blasts of dramatic music. The audience leaned forward in anticipation, not knowing whether she would be honest with her advice or selfish. In a choked whisper, trying bravely to smile, the friend breathed the admirer's name, 'Rudraksh....,' and summarized the situation in a hesitant voice. Just then, the other friend to whom she had confessed her love earlier entered the scene. But by this time, the allotted thirty minutes were over and the audience sat back again, prepared to wait till the next episode for something even more exciting to happen.

By the time Anu wound up in the kitchen, she was exhausted and irritable and in no mood to go to Nisha mausi's house the next morning to 'explain things' to Nanni.

'Why did you agree?' chided Pranab when they were getting ready for bed.

'What else could I do? You know Amma—she would have gone on and on until I agreed.'

'Well, you can try your bit, but it really isn't upto you. So don't worry whatever happens.'

'Our name will turn to mud,' said Anu gloomily. 'Like Girish Chandra Verma's. He left Patna twenty years ago, yet all anyone remembers of him is that he left because of Manvi Prasad. If Nanni becomes a famous model, I shall be forever known as the sister of a debauched body-seller!'

Pranab was used to his wife's occasional quirky pronunciations by now and ignored this outburst. 'I forgot to tell you, Shrivastava has invited us to his son's birthday party on Saturday. Do buy a gift.'

'When do I have the time to go shopping?' Anu grumbled.

'Stop somewhere on the way to Nisha mausi's house and buy something. It's his first birthday and there will be a big crowd so it doesn't matter what you pick up.'

Manvi Prasad must have enticed Girish in some way. She would have gone to his room, looking for a book, asking for advice on how to do research. She may have dropped something and bent down to pick it up. Her chunni would have fallen from her shoulders. Would he have offered to help her with her studies then? Perhaps they sat together in the college library, oblivious to the dusty shelves, tattered books and whispering students around them, shoulders knocking together, knees touching, like in the movies.

There is no place in Patna where secret lovers could meet. The whole city is crowded and people throng its public spaces and its every thoroughfare, every inch of space taken up by the frenetic activity of buying and selling, whether through a shop with stacked shelves or a plastic sheet spread on the ground. There is no room for romance.

Interlude

In the records of the Maitreyi Self-Help Group, her name was Srijana Devi. She had penned the letters herself, writing them carefully in the long register, refusing to be hurried by the energetic young woman in the starched cotton sari who represented the NGO. After all, being able to write her own name meant that she was literate and when the officer from the Sarkar came, he would put her down under the right column, even if she couldn't write anything else.

She had been called Dhaniya by her parents when she was a child. But now, she was someone's Didi, someone's Bhabhi, someone's Chachi, and Bantu ki Ma to everyone else. So when the NGO had first asked her name, she had thought for a while, then said her name was Srijana, because that was the name of the presenter of the radio programme which her husband listened to when he returned from the city. The lady in the starched cotton sari, Gauri didi, had written the name in another register and later, when they taught the women how to write their names, she had learned to copy the shapes on the slate they gave her.

But that was long ago. For many weeks, Gauri didi had come every day, in the mornings when the men were at work, and explained to them what they could do with savings. One day, she had even come with a small television set and shown them a video. It was about other women in a village like hers who had saved five rupees every month. The video showed how some of the women had bought hens, set up tea stalls, learnt tailoring or made papad with their savings and with money borrowed from the NGO. It showed how they had repaid the money and made a better life for themselves and for their children. It ended with the same group of women, now well-groomed, prosperous and laughing, happily discussing their plans in a clean and tidy village, with their clean and tidy children, dressed in proper school uniforms, smiling and playing around them, while a voice in the background said that only five rupees a month could change their lives forever.

Many women in her village had scoffed. Where would they find five rupees every month to put in a box when they didn't know where their next meal was coming from?

But Srijana Devi decided to join the group. It wasn't just the question of money. She wanted to learn how to write her name. She wanted Gauri didi to tell her how to be clean and healthy. She wanted Bantu and his siblings to look like the clean and healthy children in the film. And she wanted to buy a goat.

Gauri didi had explained that if she and the others in the group saved regularly, then after six months, they could borrow money from the NGO and buy livestock. They would look after the animals and sell them at the right time. With the money they made, they could return the NGO's loan and earn some extra money as well. Collecting that and adding more savings, they could buy more poultry or animals. It made sense to Srijana Devi.

So for many months now, she had squirrelled away a rupee or two from here and there until there was enough for the monthly meeting. Her group of fifteen women had decided to save not just five rupees, but ten rupees a month. Srijana Devi found that it was possible to hide this amount from her husband who would have otherwise spent it on alcohol. She enjoyed going for the monthly meetings. At first, she had sat a little apart because the other women were more vocal and Durga was in charge, since she could read and write a little. But now Srijana Devi, too, was an active participant. She had even gone to the bank with Gauri didi once to get their passbook updated.

After about six months, they had collected a huge amount. Gauri didi said they could choose two women to get loans of one thousand rupees each. They wrote their names on pieces of paper and put the chits into a bag. To Srijana's immense surprise, her name was one of the two drawn.

She could now buy a goat.

4

Friday

W<small>HEN</small> K<small>ALLU</small> <small>CHACHA</small> heard that Anu was going to her aunt's house, he decided to go along. 'Hum-hoon jayeb. I should go and meet Avdhesh Prasad Saran. After all, the boy's father is going to become his relative. Besides, it will save me the rickshaw fare to Kadam Kuan.'

Chachiji and Pinky were thus left to their own devices. Kallu chacha chattered with Papa in the front of the car, while Amma glowered in the back seat and Anu looked out for a suitable shop to buy the birthday present. The road was hemmed in by a line of narrow buildings, shops, houses with sagging window frames, dirty doors and unpainted walls in a variety of hues. She spotted a toy shop with plastic toys and little furry animals, tricycles and dolls covered in plastic, balls and guns, all hanging from nails hammered into the outer wall.

She asked Papa to stop the car. The shop, little more than a hole in the wall, had already encroached onto the street with its display of colourful toys, as had all other shops, and there was no real space available for the car. The vehicles behind them, the usual mix of handcarts, bicycles, motorcycles, rickshaws, vans, cars and other miscellaneous modes of transport, protested with a blaring of horns and ringing of bells when the ancient Fiat slowed down. Anu asked Papa to stop a little further on, but Amma said, 'What does it matter! We are only stopping for a few minutes, Papa will have to go onto the street again. Go and buy your present jaldi-jaldi.'

Anu quickly barged into the shop, selected a furry animal with blank hard eyes, and went to the counter to pay. The shopkeeper was busy with another customer who was taking her time to choose from little plastic cooking utensils. By this time, the traffic had adjusted to the impediment on the road and was snaking its way slowly and stoically around Papa's car. While the customer debated over the blue pan and the pink pot, Anu asked the shopkeeper to take her money. 'Can't you see I am busy! Wait for your turn,' he snapped at her.

Amma, watching from the car with the window rolled down, yelled at him, 'Jaldi karo, bhaiyya! You have usurped half the road, there is no place left to park and everyone is honking at us. Do you want the police to come here?'

The shopkeeper took quick stock of the situation and sullenly took Anu's money. Anu grabbed the furry animal and rushed back to the car, slamming the door after her. Papa turned the key, there was a screeching sound but the engine did not start.

'Maybe there are too many people in the car and it has become heavy,' Amma suggested with a baleful glance at Kallu chacha, so they all exited the vehicle except Papa, who continued to fiddle with the key, the choke and the accelerator. People were stopping to stare. Kallu chacha looked a few of the young men in the eye and said, 'Ka ho! Will someone push the car or not? I would have pushed it myself if it wasn't for my heart problem.'

Anu still had the furry animal in her hands. She tossed it through the car window onto the seat. Three intrepid young men heeded Kallu chacha's call and pushed the car, while a crowd gathered to watch the proceedings. There was hardly any space for the car to move, but somehow they managed to accelerate the car for a few metres. The engine caught, thankfully, and rumbled to life. The young men stood back with triumphant smiles and Papa leaned out of the window and thanked them for their help. Amma, Kallu chacha and Anu took their places in the car again, and they drove off at a sedate pace.

The furry animal was no longer on the seat.

Amma wanted to stop and question the crowd, but Anu said the car might not start again, they wouldn't be able to find the thief, and she would just give some money to the birthday boy. Amma protested that they couldn't let money go waste like this, but Kallu chacha pointed out that they should be going to the mechanic to see what the problem was with the car or they would be stuck on the road again. So Amma abandoned her plans of looking for the thief, satisfying herself instead with a general diatribe about the ills of a criminal society which were only to be expected with politicians like these. Fortunately, just then they found themselves outside a tiny shop down the road where a mechanic was persuaded to open the hood of the car and take a peek at its innards.

'Car has become too hot,' proclaimed the specialist, a teenager covered in motor oil from head to toe. 'Needs servicing.'

'We can't give it for servicing now, bhaiyya,' said Papa. 'Can't you do something so that it doesn't stop?'

The boy shrugged, then poured a canful of water into the radiator. The radiator hissed and steamed. 'Keep adding water,' the boy advised sternly. 'But get it serviced soon.'

Papa gave him twenty rupees, they all piled into the car and joined the stream of traffic once more.

'You gave him too much money,' Amma protested.

The rest of the journey was spent talking about Gautam. Apparently, he had had a 'love marriage' with a baniya girl in Delhi, much to the chagrin of his parents. However, as their other son had settled in the US, the parents were in the unhappy position of having to live with the ex-caste daughter-in-law. It seemed the girl even had some kind of a mental problem which made her take to her bed at regular intervals, thus keeping her from the household tasks which her ailing mother-in-law was forced to undertake. Most of all, even after several years of marriage, the unfortunate girl had been unable to produce an issue, male or otherwise. Gautam was now in Patna for a holiday, although why anyone would want to come to Patna for a holiday when they had no close relatives here was a much-debated mystery. It was a good thing Kallu chacha had run into Gautam on the street and could give him company.

'Ladka theek-ay ba,' Kallu chacha proclaimed and, for a change, Amma had to agree with this judgement.

Before further details about Gautam's life could be

discussed, Nisha mausi's decrepit old house came into view, and Amma and Kallu chacha had to regretfully abandon their amicable banter.

Preparations for the engagement ceremony were in chaotic flow. Nisha mausi was sitting on a green cane chair in the veranda, clutching a notebook and chewing on a pen. The cook, bespoke for the momentous occasion in a dirty dhoti and undershirt, sat on his haunches near her feet, a black thread round his neck testifying to his Brahmin credentials. They were ostensibly discussing the menu and the groceries that needed to be purchased, but were continually interrupted by valuable suggestions from Nisha mausi's sister-in-law, seated strategically close by.

'Ka ho! How can you think of alu-parwal curry at this time! Don't you know the parwal in the market is very ripe and hard and the seeds are like stones? Better to have alu-lauki instead.'

'He is making lauki kofta, Didiji,' Nisha mausi pointed out hesitatingly.

'That is the problem in this season,' Didiji sat back, her nose wrinkled distastefully. 'There are no vegetables in the market. This is why people don't like to have ceremonies at this time of year.'

Amma strode up the stairs to the veranda. 'Kyon, kya hua? Can the girl's family dictate to the boy's family the date for the engagement? Every function in this season has alu-parwal, Maharaj will just have to buy the parwal carefully.'

The cook tittered uncomfortably. 'Didiji knows for such a big function it is impossible to look at every single parwal. There will always be hard seeds.'

'You tell your boys to pick them out when they are cutting the vegetables then. Ek-ek tho beej-va nikaaley ke padi!' Didiji commanded, her tone implying dire consequences if even a single seed was found in the entire patila of curry. 'So now you have alu-parwal, lauki kofta and paneer-matar, then dahi-bada, tomato chutney, pulao, papad. And chicken curry for the non-vegetarians...'

'Paneer-matar?' Amma interrupted. 'You know that will be very costly in this season. You should have paneer kofta; you can mix in potatoes and bread and use less paneer that way. No one can tell the difference.'

The cook shifted on his haunches. 'It does not taste as good.'

'As if you care! You just want to make more money on the paneer. Make paneer kofta, alu-parwal and lauki-chana curry. That is plenty for this occasion.'

Having finalized everything and leaving the minor details to Didiji and Nisha mausi, Amma made her way indoors. Papa and Kallu chacha were sitting with Avdhesh Prasad Saran in the drawing room. Kallu chacha had already begun expounding on the ills of having a daughter of marriageable age and what a trial it was for him to tread up and down two states looking for a prospective groom. Papa and old Mr Saran listened respectfully—Papa sitting carefully on the edge of the sofa, Mr Saran shrivelled up in the big armchair that had always comfortably accommodated his frame. Amma paid her respects perfunctorily to Mr Saran, and stood for a minute to inform him, the head of the household, about the arrangements she had made for the engagement, while Kallu chacha, interrupted in full flow, glowered at her.

'But Samdhinji, lauki-chana is not so good for an important ceremony like this!' he finally interjected.

'It's okay for an engagement,' Amma said dismissively. 'Now I have to go and meet my niece.'

Amma pushed aside the curtain hanging from a string in the doorway and walked into the central part of the house, a large room with cracked red cement flooring and flaking green walls, furnished with some string-cots, a pockmarked table and a few straight-backed chairs. The room had not been done up in a quarter century. It was presently occupied by Tullu, Didiji's youngest son, who was sprawled on one of the cots reading a Hindi film magazine. Amma ignored him and made straight for another doorway, calling Nanni's name as she went. Anu followed behind, giving Tullu a friendly smile to make up for her mother's rudeness.

Nanni got up from the bed when Amma and Anu entered the room. Anu was so shocked to see the change in the girl that she stopped in her tracks at the door.

A year ago, Nanni was an awkward adolescent, all bony arms and flat chest, oily hair in long plaits hanging over skinny shoulders, eyes a little too large peering somewhat uncomprehendingly at the world. While her dark skin had always been a cause of anxiety, her height had also become a source of tension as it further narrowed her marriage prospects. Dressed always in shapeless salwar-kameezes that had been discarded by her elder sisters, Nanni had been easily relegated to an unobtrusive presence in her large family. Brilliant like her unfortunate father, but studious unlike him, she had ultimately secured, without much effort, the necessary high marks that ensured her a place in one of Delhi's prestigious colleges. Her uncle was no longer able to avoid a posting outside Delhi, so Nanni was sent to live in a hostel.

That appeared to have been her undoing. According to Amma, the close companionship with unsuitable girls, the undisciplined freedom of college, the contact with a culture totally different from her experience, and other such extremely unsatisfactory developments had transformed her. The change had not been as evident during her last visit to Patna, though Amma had even then insisted on lecturing the girl about the moral values she was expected to live by even if she now lived in the country's capital. And now here she was, a tall lissome teenager with smooth dusky skin, a slim, graceful body, shiny dark hair attractively dishevelled around high cheekbones, sparkling eyes darkly outlined with kajal—looking almost as though she had just stepped out from a photo-shoot, a confident, successful model. She wore a pair of pink cotton pants and a kurti, a tiny silver chain drawing attention to the long neck, a simple pair of stone earrings dangling against her straight jaw line.

Is this the same child who came crying to me one morning because no one took notice of her any more and her Papa was not there to make her feel better? My days of looking good are long over.

'Pranam, Lata mausi, pranam, Anu di,' Nanni came forward to touch their feet, smiling with genuine pleasure at seeing them.

'Khush raho, Nanni. How were your exams?' Amma asked.

'They were okay, Mausi. We'll know when the results are out, won't we?'

'Very good, very good.' Amma actually looked discomfited, as though she, always the mistress of any occasion, was at a loss for words. 'So... well, you never had any problems with exams, you have always been so good at studies, like your Anu di, except she never studied as much as you. When does college reopen?'

'In mid-July. But I have to go a little earlier,' Nanni replied, lounging back onto the bed, hugging her knees, drawing attention to her perfect little rounded bottom and slender arms. Anu winced, but Amma didn't seem to notice.

There was half an instant of silence, while Amma wavered. Then she said, 'Kyon, kya hua? Your mother needs you here to prepare for the wedding.'

'I need to train for a shoot.' She sat up, her eyes glowing with sudden excitement. 'Mausi, it's the most wonderful opportunity! It's a new fruit drink that is being launched and they selected me after seeing my photos. I even had to appear for a screen test. The agency is going to train us, and then select one of us for the campaign.'

'Fruit drink!' Amma exclaimed. Her face contorted, but she decided not to tackle Nanni at this stage. In persuasion, she was the weapon of last resort, the final word when all others failed, as happened only too often. 'Anu di has something important to say to you. I have to go and see what the cook is doing—he will probably make Nishu buy four times the supplies she needs. Anu, talk to Nanni,' and with that imperious command she swept out of the room, leaving the dirty work to her daughter.

Anu seated herself on the bed across from Nanni. 'It sounds like a really great break. Which ad agency is it?'

'It's a new place; it's been set up by some people who used to work for Trikaya Gray which is a really good multinational ad agency.'

'Have they done much other work?'

'I don't really know. Basically, they have just started out, but they've managed to get this really good client who is setting up the fruit drink company.'

'Are they serious about you or are you just another prospect?'

'I know what you're thinking.' Nanni's face turned sullen. 'But they're not like that. They are really decent guys. I mean, one can tell, Anu di. There is another girl from my college and a couple of others from other places and they're all excited about it. I mean, one good ad can make your career.'

'But are you sure you want a career in modelling? You are so bright, you could easily do an MBA.'

'I can always do that later. But if I become famous, there will be so many options available to me, and money won't be a problem anymore. I'll have so much money I won't know what to do with it!'

'Well, good luck then. I hope you do get chosen for the campaign. I, for one, will be very proud to see your face all over the country!'

Anu got up from the bed. She felt she had done the duty entrusted to her by her mother. She had not exactly dissuaded Nanni from a modelling career, but she was sure her few well-chosen questions would create doubts in her mind and force her to examine her options more closely. Given the uncertainty hanging over the matter, it was highly unlikely that Nanni's face would be plastered on billboards across the country. Amma could save herself, and others, a lot of needless anxiety if she stopped blowing things out of proportion. Anu walked out of the room, determined to leave soon; it was time for the children to come back from school.

However, returning home was not destined to be so easy. Despite her protests, Anu found herself invited to stay for lunch along with her parents, Didiji and even Kallu chacha, whose objections were quite feeble and not meant to be taken seriously as everyone knew there was no other place in the vicinity to which he could repair for lunch. As for the children, Amma reminded her, Chachiji and Pinky were home to look after them, weren't they.

Before lunch was served on huge stainless-steel thalis and handed to the men, Anu managed to call home and was much heartened by Arnab's ill-tempered protest at her not being present. She promised, quite audibly for the benefit of the others, to be back home as soon as possible. Then she poured out drinking water from the large earthenware pot with a long stainless-steel ladle into oversized stainless-steel glasses and set them in front of the men sitting at the pockmarked table. The meal went by mostly in silence—Papa and Mr Saran had little in common, and Kallu chacha was, for once, too busy enjoying his meal to say anything. Tullu, still devouring his magazine, asked for more rice and vegetables and Nanni fetched the bowls from the dim kitchen. She ladled out more rice and dal for all the men, while Anu went around the table with curry and bhujia.

Eventually, Kallu chacha burped violently and washed his hand with water from his glass, letting it pour into the thali, as he looked around meaningfully for something sweet to follow. Nanni hurriedly fetched him a big stainless-steel bowl of dahi and sugar which he polished off with great relish, scraping the spoon against the bowl to get at every last grain of sugar. Then, without waiting for the others to finish, he made his way to the sink and, with a mugful of water from the plastic bucket under it, rinsed his mouth and cleared his throat, making a fair amount of unseemly noise in the process.

I wonder how people rinse their mouths in America. What if he expects a fork and knife for his meals? And paper napkins!

When the men left the table, the little servant-boy gathered the thalis, washed them and laid them, dripping wet, back on the table. After that the elderly female relatives sat down to eat, Didiji and Amma vying with one another to list the things that still needed to be assembled for the engagement, including gold rings for the groom and the bride. This led to a heated discussion on how Western ways had overtaken Indian customs. Why, in the old days, the girl wasn't even supposed to be present at her engagement, her family could just go with fruits and gifts and 'book' the boy, and then, if the boy's side so wished, they—only the immediate family, of course—could come and fill the girl's lap with rice and a handful of dried fruits and partake of lavish hospitality. How everything had changed now, exchanging rings and displaying the girl and expecting a huge function to entertain all kinds of people, including distant acquaintances!

By the time Anu and Nanni sat down to eat, it was late afternoon and when Papa dropped Anu home, with everyone in the car anticipating another breakdown at any moment and making him so nervous that he could barely inch along, it was almost tea-time.

Chachiji had already woken from her afternoon nap and the children were busy playing cards with Pinky bua.

'Aa gaeel! So you are back at last! I waited and waited. Your maid also came. She was in a hurry, there was some problem with her daughter's engagement. We hadn't eaten when she came, so she couldn't do the dishes. You know what she said? She said Maiji could do them herself, because she had to go. So we hurriedly ate lunch and I told her to wash the dishes before she left. She broke two glasses. I scolded her but she is really impertinent and wouldn't listen when I told her to be careful.'

Chachiji was clearly determined to go on about what a horrible maid Anu had, but Anu was in no mood to listen. She mumbled something about the bathroom and dashed off to her room.

Fortunately, Arnab distracted her by telling her that there was a message for her.

Dear Anuradha,

I can't imagine how everyone knows about my visit. And what exactly is the reason that I left? As far as I know, I applied for a PhD, got a scholarship, borrowed money from my brother, and went.

I hope your uncle-in-law will not mind sharing space with me. Please do let me know if I can bring something for him or if you need anything from here. How old are your children? Is there anything I can bring for them?

Looking forward to hearing from you.

Best,
Girish

Anu felt sorry for the professor; he was trying to hide the fact that he had had to leave because of a scandal. It was a shameful thing, to be thrown out of the university for being in love with a student.

'Mummy, tell him to bring me some Pokemon. And a computer game. Harsh's father brought him five CDs when he went to America!'

'We can't ask an unknown guest to bring gifts, Golu. It's not polite.'

'Okay,' replied Arnab, with the fortitude of one who had not expected his request to be met anyway. 'Do you want to reply?'

'Just tell me how it's done.'

'You won't understand, Mummy. See, first click on "Reply", then type your letter, then click on "Send". To switch off the computer, you have to click on "Start", then "Shut down". To turn on...'

'Okay, never mind. I'll call you when I need help.'

Dear Sir,

I am grateful for your offer to bring something from America, but we do not require anything from there.

Kallu chacha is here to discuss a marriage proposal for his daughter. It is a doctor from Arrah. I think there is little chance the matter will work out, and I am sure he will leave before your arrival. Pinky is a very nice girl, but dowry demands are very high these days. I don't think Kallu chacha can afford a doctor. Since nobody wants to tell him he is setting his hopes too high, he continues to waste time here.

I have a daughter who is fourteen years old and a son who is nine. But they do not need anything from there either.

Thank you very much for asking.

With kind regards,
Anuradha

The message sent, Anuradha went to rest.

She woke up with a start when she heard Pranab's voice.

'What happened? Are you ill?' Pranab was surprised to see her still in bed at 6.30.

Anu hurriedly sat up and grabbed her comb. 'No, no. I'm fine. We got back from Nisha mausi's house very late and I must have been quite tired. Where are the children?'

'Golu has gone out to play and Radhika is talking on the phone. What took you so long there?'

'They insisted we have lunch with them. Kallu chacha was quite happy to stay on as he didn't seem to have any work and Amma also wanted to discuss the arrangements for the ceremony. I think she has got everything in hand now.'

'Isn't there anyone in Nisha mausi's family to take care of all that? How come it's all Amma's responsibility?'

'You know how it is. The men will only arrive on the day of the ceremony and Amma... I'd better get you your tea.'

'Don't worry. Pinky is making it.' Pranab returned to the living room to sit with Kallu chacha.

Anu dragged the comb through her hair furiously. It was bad enough having unexpected guests. Did they have to take over her kitchen as well?

When Arnab returned from his match, Anu realized she had been looking forward to his arrival so he could tell her if she had any new mail. It was wonderful to have a stranger send her messages instantaneously over such a distance. She had heard of people using computers to buy tickets, to talk to their children abroad or even to check on their grandchildren in the US through cameras, but she herself had not yet discovered its delights. For housewives like herself, there was not much use for a computer, unless to take recipes from the internet. The contact with a stranger seemed to open her up.

There was a message.

Dear Anuradha,

Some things in Patna have obviously not changed. My deepest sympathies for Kallu chacha and Pinky.

I am doing some research on society, culture and identity, with special reference to gender and family relations in non-metro Indian cities and am coming to Patna for case studies such as Pinky's. I would like to meet a cross-section of women, including working women, for this purpose. While I had thought to identify potential subjects after my arrival, it seems to me that you may be able to help start the process.

I would be immensely grateful if you could draw up a list of women in your society that I could meet with. The subjects preferably should be from varied age groups and income levels.

My project is funded and I would be happy to reimburse you for your efforts.

I look forward to your positive reply.

Best,
Girish

P.S. Which Transformer would your son like to have?

Amma was right! Girish sir wanted to be alone with women.

That was silly, Anu chided herself as she tried to think rationally. Nobody would come all the way to Patna to assault women.

There was no mention of family problems and ancient quarrels in the message. No lost loves either. Was the purpose of the long overdue visit really official? She would now have to consult Pranab about Girish sir's request. But she sat at the desk and clicked on 'Reply'.

Dear Sir,

I would be happy to help you find the subjects for your research, although unfortunately my relatives and friends are mostly from the Kayastha community. My mother knows a lot of people in Patna and I could ask her for names. You could also meet my cousin who is keen on becoming a model in Delhi, though my mother thinks that will be bad for our family's reputation and is trying to dissuade her. I myself don't think there is anything wrong with being a model in these times. There is a lot of money in it and girls find the profession very glamorous. However, I am not sure I would like Radhika, my daughter, to become a model.

I will send you a list later. Would you like me to include Bhumihars, Rajputs, Kurmis, Koeris and other castes as well? I could get names from Pranab. Thank you for offering to reimburse me, but I cannot accept that.

With kind regards,
Anu

The reply came before Anu could recall Arnab's instructions about how to switch off the computer.

Dear Anu,

Thanks for your quick reply and your willingness to help. I really appreciate it.

It is 6 a.m. here in New Jersey, so forgive me if I sound a little bleary. Your mother sounds very traditional, but I must be conservative as well. I seem to agree with her about not letting your cousin become a model. I suppose one can never get away from one's background no matter how much one tries to lose one's self in another culture and in another country.

I look forward to your list. Keep it to your relatives and friends for now. Thanks again.

Have a nice day.
Girish

Anu read the mail a few times. When she went to bed, the lines about losing one's self remained in her head and she wondered what it must feel like, to be so much in love with a person that one could not bear to be near and yet apart. In an arranged marriage, the husband and wife got used to each other, learnt to love each other over time, sharing lives, taking delight in children, doing things together... There was no sudden, tumultuous assault on the emotions, no all-consuming passion, no powerful tug of unbearable attraction. But love... love could be strong enough to persuade someone to leave everything familiar and start a new life.

What exactly does that feel like?

5

Saturday

SATURDAYS WERE HALF-DAYS at the bank and the schools were closed. Chachiji, an early riser, switched on the TV for the dawn bhajans while she went about her ablutions. During the week, the clanging of cymbals and the monotonous drone had little effect on Anu, but today it was the signal for her to get up. It would be extremely unseemly to lounge in bed while a senior relative was awake and pottering around, though it was barely light outside. By the time she washed her face, combed her hair and went out, Chachiji was trying to wake up the children. It was evening in New Jersey.

'Jaldi utha-ho. The bus will be coming soon. Radhika, get up, beta! Golu, get up, you are getting late!'

'Let them sleep, Chachiji. The school is closed on Saturday,' Anu reminded her.

'Closed? In our days, we went to school six days a week.'

'Would you like your tea now or a little later?'

'You know I have to have my tea now or I won't be able to go to the toilet. As it is my bowel is a little disturbed this morning as I waited too long for my lunch yesterday when you all didn't return; I had to take a Digene yesterday. Ae, Pinky, tani chai lava-ho. Go help Bhabhi with the tea.'

Thus having absolved herself of guilt, if any, about being an infliction, Chachiji sat in front of the TV and hummed along with the bhajan tunelessly. The song ended and a saffron-clad sadhu with the mandatory smear of ash on his forehead took over. 'It is all the will of the Mother,' he intoned. 'You will be whatever She wants you to be. She wants you all to be good persons. She wants you all to be good to people around you. She wants you to be good to the plants and animals around you. If you make people unhappy, if you make people sad, if you make people angry, if you disturb the plants and animals, She will make you suffer. For, after all, She is the Mother and the Mother always punishes children who do not obey Her. The Mother loves you but She will berate those who do not follow Her wishes. So you must all try and make Her happy just as you try to make your own mothers happy. So let us all sing...'

Anu thought about leaving the children with Chachiji and Pinky and asking Pranab to drop her off for shopping. The list of items she needed to purchase to prepare for her guest from America buzzed around in her mind and she had to force herself to calm down.

But before she could outline her plans to anyone, it transpired that Kallu chacha already had plans to visit Chachiji's cousin in Pataliputra Colony. He expected Pranab to drive them to the Boring Road crossing, and although it was a considerable distance out of the way for him, Pranab was not complaining, thankful that Chachaji had not asked him for a lift all the way to Pataliputra. Being accommodative and considerate, Kallu chacha intended to catch an auto from Boring Road. But going all the way by auto would take too long. Besides, there might not be any autos available nearby and Chachiji could hardly be expected to walk in search of one, given her knee pain. That's the end of my shopping, thought Anu gloomily, and went to prepare breakfast

Since the children were home and she didn't have to spend time on packing lunches, breakfast on Saturdays tended to be more elaborate than usual. Pinky couldn't help her as she was busy fetching and carrying for her parents while they got dressed, and then had to get ready herself, as leaving with Pranab meant they had to be ready by a certain time. But Anu did not miss the help in the kitchen as she was looking forward to a whole day without Chachiji, Kallu chacha and Pinky to cater to. It was only to be expected that Chachiji's cousin would provide lunch for the visitors. She wondered what people in America did on weekends. Surely they would not spend their time cooking extra in case people dropped in.

Anu's other task for the morning was to prepare Arnab for his weekly test on Wednesday. This week it was mathematics and Anu struggled to explain the concepts of denominators, numerators and equivalent fractions to her son who appeared never to have heard of these terms before.

Really, do they teach anything at all in schools these days?

Radhika, who had Hindi this week, flounced out of the room, complaining loudly that with guests in the house and Anu yelling at Arnab, it was impossible to study. She shut herself in Anu's room with her pile of books and did not emerge till lunchtime.

Anu's own unexpected visitor that morning was Anita from downstairs who panted up the stairs to borrow the iron as hers was not working. Setting Arnab some problems from the practice book she had bought at the beginning of the school year, Anu politely offered her tea. Anita accepted readily, despite the fact that she could see Anu was busy teaching her son. She made herself comfortable on the sofa, helped herself to a glucose biscuit, dipped it into the tea and stuffed it into her mouth, then asked about the family members, including Kallu chacha whom she had seen going down with Pranab.

'What match are they looking at this time?' she enquired, aware that Kallu chacha frequently came to Patna in search of a groom for Pinky.

'There is a doctor in Arrah whose father is coming for Gunni's engagement. Kallu chacha met his uncle in Ranchi.'

'These doctors always want medico girls. Pinky is only a graduate, hai na?'

'She has done computer courses also in Ranchi.'

'Arre, what computer job can you get in a place like Arrah?' Anita said dismissively. 'Kallu chacha is wasting his time on this doctor! Besides, he'll have to give so much dowry.'

'Chachaji says this boy does not want any dowry.'

'Phir bhi, there is so much expense for the wedding ceremony itself and for setting up the house.'

'That is always there.'

'Anyway, I'm sure Pinky will find a match one of these days. Who can say anything about marriages? They are fixed by the gods themselves. But what about Nanni?'

'Nanni is too young for us to think about her marriage. There is still Manni to worry about after Gunni is settled,' Anu prevaricated, hoping Anita had not heard about Nanni's plans.

But she had.

'Not many men in our kinds of families would want to marry a girl who has been a model,' said Anita in a conspiratorial tone. So much for Amma's aspirations to keep it under wraps. 'My niece, whose friend studies in Nanni's college, told me that Nanni has been selected for some modelling competition. My niece also wanted to go for that competition but thankfully, she is not as tall as Nanni, although she is much fairer and has nice sharp features. And her complexion is almost milky-white. She may be a little plump, but she comes from a prosperous family. Nowadays all young girls want to become models. It is up to us elders to correct them. Otherwise, shaadi-vaadi kaise hogi, na?'

'I don't know about that. I think girls should be able to do whatever they are good at, and Nanni is so bright she can easily go to one of the IIMs. Then there will be no marriage problem even if she does become a model. Besides, once she is a top model, she may find her own husband, maybe even a filmstar or a cricketer.'

Anita tittered disbelievingly. 'Well, anyway, hum chalte hain. I need to cook lunch. I'll send the iron back with the maid.'

Anu understood now why Anita's iron was not working. 'Be sure to send it back early,' she told Anita reprovingly. 'I need it for a dinner we are going to this evening.'

For a moment, she thought Anita would quiz her on the details of the dinner, but fortunately, lunchtime was rather close so she refrained and made her way downstairs.

The maid rang the bell at quarter past eleven, when Anu had all but given up hope and was ready to do the dishes and leave out the sweeping and swabbing altogether.

'Late again! Why can't you ever come on time? And when we want you to come late you turn up early, before anyone has even had lunch. Chachiji was very upset with you yesterday.'

'Hai, ka karein! Maiji, you will not believe the trouble I have been put through because of that unfortunate eldest daughter of mine!' the maid exclaimed, throwing her hands up dramatically.

'Kyon, kya hua?'

'Arre, ask what did not happen! You remember my eldest daughter's engagement, na? You will not believe what happened when they came! Tabah-tabah ho gaeeni!'

'What? How did they trouble you?' asked Anu.

'The boy's mother, father, brother and he himself come to our house carrying clothes and sweets. I sit them down and give them sharbat and fried papad. Then they want me to bring out the girl to start the ceremony. So I go and bring her, she is nicely dressed in a new salwar suit with sequins. Her younger sisters come in with her. The boy's mother raises the ghunghat for tika. And suddenly she is shouting and shouting! We say, calm down and tell us what happened, but she keeps on screaming. Then her husband tells her to shut up and tell us the problem. And then, Maiji, she says this was not the girl they saw earlier and that we switched girls! I said, Bakwaas ba! What nonsense! This is the same girl, my elder daughter, whom you approved a week ago. She says she has eyes in her head, she is not some batty old woman to let us dupe her. She points to my second daughter and says, this is the girl she saw last week. Then I also got angry. I told her how dare she say I was cheating and why would I show her my second daughter when the first was not yet married. She said it was because the second daughter was prettier—and that's true, Maiji, she has taken after me but my eldest has taken after her father. So we all yelled and yelled at each other. Then they took the clothes and sweets and left.'

By now, Anu was weary of this interminable story, but seeing that the maid was not yet finished, she tuned her out.

'How could I bear this injustice? How dare that woman accuse me of switching girls? Dikha deyeeni okhra! This morning, I marched to her house, taking my eldest daughter with me. In front of all her neighbours and relatives, I told her she was a miserable suspicious old woman who was going back on her word. She had agreed to marry her son to my eldest daughter but when she saw the younger one, she changed her mind and was now trying to grab her. I told her the eldest daughter is such a skilled, hardworking young girl, she would be a bigger asset than the other one who often falls sick. So what if she is not as pretty as her sister? I also said that god would punish her for choosing outer beauty over inner beauty. Finally, she called me into the house and both of us sat there and the boy also came and talked to my daughter and in the end, I persuaded them not to break the match. I even promised to help with a new rickshaw, then we...'

'Good, so it is all settled then. Now go do your work, it is already very late.'

The maid headed for the kitchen but continued to expound on the salient points of her morning's triumph to an invisible audience. Anu checked in on Radhika, who refused to be mollified, and hurried back to Arnab and his sums.

Unfortunately, while Arnab was still struggling to grasp the theories, the doorbell rang again. Hurriedly, Anu charged Arnab with completing the sums in Exercise 1 (i) a to e, and rushed to open the door, knowing full well that he would never get beyond the first one.

It was Gautam. Surprised, Anu invited him in.

'Is Pranab bhaiyya here?' he asked as he stepped in. He looked rather perturbed and uncertain.

'Kallu chacha has gone to meet your Babua mama,' she replied absent-mindedly, hoping to get rid of him before Arnab was distracted from his studies for the third time that morning. 'Oh! Bhaiyya! No, he is at the bank, but he should be back any minute. It's almost lunchtime.'

'May I wait for him?'

'Yes. Please sit,' she indicated the sofa. Politely, she seated herself across on the armchair and tried to make small talk.

'How is your wife? She is not visiting Patna with you?'

'Yes, she is also here,' replied Gautam. There was a pause while Anu tried to think of the next question.

'You have come to Patna for a holiday?'

'No, not a holiday.'

Anu was hoping to get to the real reason for his stay here, but his answer did not give away anything. His father was from UP, and his mother was from Muzaffarpur, so maybe it was some mandatory family function that he had come for? But that did not explain his aura of restlessness and doubt.

'A marriage then?'

Gautam stood up abruptly and walked to the window, as Anu watched, bewildered.

When he turned towards her, his eyes were focused and intent. 'My wife is not too well. I thought a change of scene would do her good. I used to come here quite often when my grandparents were alive. I wanted her to see my past.'

'She has not been to Patna before?'

'No, she is from Delhi,' he replied. He paced back to the sofa. 'What is that sound?'

It was Arnab, already lobbing a ball at the walls.

The tense air around Gautam evaporated suddenly. Flashing a quick smile at Anu, he strode into the bedroom and picked up Arnab's textbook, while Anu gaped from the doorway. 'Hmm, fractions. Denominators, numerators and terminators?'

Arnab giggled and threw the ball at him. Gautam caught it easily and tossed it into a corner. 'Denominators are the clever underdogs, they are under the line, but they dominate. They all have to be the same, isn't it?'

'Yes,' agreed Arnab, delighted to have this opportunity to share his new knowledge. 'You have to find the LCM, then multiply the numbers at the top, and only then can you add or subtract!'

'See? You know it all.' He handed back the book. 'Bet you can't solve all the problems, though, they look really complicated.'

And it was as simple as that. Arnab was back at the table, ready to take up the challenge.

'Mummy is talking online to a professor in America!' he announced as he opened his book. 'She e-mails him every day! He is coming to stay with us from the twenty-first.'

'Achha? Interesting. Do you think he knows fractions?'

Arnab laughed at this. 'No, he is a sociology professor, he doesn't know maths!'

'Maybe I will come and visit him when he comes.'

Mortified at this exposure, Anu glared at her son as Gautam returned to the living room.

'I have to go now, but I will come again later,' Gautam told Anu. 'It was nothing important anyway.'

'Do bring your wife. We'd love to meet her,' Anu mumbled politely, wanting to thank him, not knowing how.

After the problems had been dealt with, Anu got Arnab to show her how to switch on the computer and access the e-mail account. There were no new messages so she wrote one herself.

Dear Sir,

I have been thinking about your list. Another woman you could interview is my maid who has six daughters and is having another baby soon. She earns very little money and is trying to get her eldest daughter engaged but she is facing problems. I will tell you the story once you are here. Poor women here have no thought for their future. Maybe you can explain this to me since you are a sociology professor. Also, why are some women so curious about the details of other women's lives? Why should it matter to my neighbour if Kallu chacha's daughter gets married or not, or if Nanni becomes a model?

Kallu chacha has gone to visit a relative. What do you do in America if you don't have family to visit?

Anu

Anu peered hopefully at the monitor for a few minutes and shortly, the message icon flashed.

Dear Anu,

Your maid sounds like the perfect subject and I can hardly wait to hear the story of her daughter's engagement. The ecostructure of a society encourages convergence of individual choice with the parameters determined by the majority. Then there are exceptions like me who retain their unique identities in different network matrices. Consequently, we will be out of sync with whichever society we are associated.

Your neighbour's relationship networks extend beyond her immediate relatives. Her behaviour is typical in a society where a web of concentric circles of relationships heavily influences the individual's self-identity. In some societies such as here, these circles are separate rather than intersecting, and the individual's sense of self is therefore distinct. In case you are interested, I attach a few website addresses that you might view.

What do I do with no family to visit? Good question. My son, fifteen years old, lives in California, so I see him only during summer vacations. I actually don't have time to do many things I would like to do because of work pressure. I read a lot, surf the net, write papers. More when I come.

Best,
Girish

Pranab came in just then. Anu hurriedly turned off the computer and told him about Gautam's visit. 'I wonder what he wanted,' Pranab mused. 'I barely know him.'

6

Gautam's Story

As Gautam walked down the dim staircase, he wondered why he had not waited for Pranab bhaiyya. Although he had met him just once, he felt he could rely on him for good advice. Patna itself was unfamiliar, childhood memories now distorted, but it was the best place for his present purposes. He was impatient to resolve Megha's problem now that he had the solution.

It was like a sea of cold black oil, thick, dark, viscous, with no sunlight bouncing off its surface, no silver beams at night. It was constant, and it was unyielding, and it was relentless. It threatened her all the time, and he could see the effort she put in to keep the roiling black oil at the edges of her consciousness.

And then sometimes, she tired of the effort and he felt the thick oil seep through the cracks in her mind, through the protective walls she had erected within, slowly staining the surfaces, then spreading ever faster till it obliterated that part of her which thought, triumphantly burying it in heavy darkness. And still it kept streaming through, until it succeeded in drowning her in the sluggish blackness, until the cold froze her thoughts and lethargy crept over her. And then she would lie in bed, staring up with blank, soulless eyes that didn't see, didn't care, didn't want, didn't live. It seemed to Gautam that it was he, not she, who fought against the blackness that enveloped her. Her constrictions made him claustrophobic.

That was why that trip to the southern tea estates a few months ago had been so important. As his managers would have put it, it was a game-changer.

It was an early November morning in Delhi, cool and clear. But in Cochin, it was already a balmy day. The air-conditioning in the car insulated him from the outside and he felt that the coconut trees and the long, straight road were not his world. The long car journey from the airport allowed him to thrust aside the files and reports he had been studying during the flight, and to think about Megha. She had been lying in bed when he said goodbye, but she was back in her darkness and did not hear him.

Gautam thought back to their college days, when he had first met Megha. He had been serious and studious, conscious of his responsibility to his family and trying to do the best he could. But for Megha's parents, college was merely a necessary qualification for marriage, not a stepping stone to a career. She was the youngest of four daughters, three of whom had been successfully married off by their traditional father into other traditional families. But Megha was different. She had worked hard and emerged with excellent grades and good job offers. He remembered with a smile the struggles they both had to face in their families where such things as 'love marriages' were not condoned. For several years they persisted, refused to consider other options, until they finally won over the elders. Then the wrangling over rituals began. If they couldn't choose their children's spouses, at least they could maintain their own traditions during the wedding ceremonies.

The first obstacle was over who should call on whom to discuss the details. The boy's family insisted that the girl's parents humbly appear before them as was customary. The girl's parents, on the other hand, already upset about having to face the ignominy of an inter-caste marriage for their daughter, expected the boy's parents to formally ask for their daughter's hand. The problem was finally resolved by Gautam who presented himself regularly at Megha's house. Through assiduous polite conversation and avoidance of all even remotely controversial topics, he finally managed to convince her parents that he was a worthy son-in-law even though he was of a different caste. A compromise was effected by having Gautam's cousin and his wife call on Megha's parents, after which they agreed at last to meet Gautam's parents.

Further problems were encountered when astrologers were consulted separately for the wedding date. Both family astrologers agreed only on one thing—that the marriage was an inauspicious union, given the position of the stars at the times of birth of bride and groom.

Terrible things would happen to them and, more importantly, to their families, if they married. The exact nature of the impending misfortunes could not definitely be predicted by either of them but it would certainly be calamitous. Gautam had to secretly bestow monetary favours on both astrologers before they conceded that they might just have miscalculated their charts and could give a mutually agreed auspicious date, not too far away in the future, for the wedding to take place.

Another contretemps ensued when Megha's father despatched the usual household articles to Gautam's house a few days before the wedding. Under normal circumstances, Gautam's family, although too cultured to actually demand dowry, would nevertheless have presented the prospective bride's family with a wish list of gift items. But the unforeseen arrival of huge ornate furniture and gleaming new appliances was viewed as an insult, as an exhibitionist display of wealth.

'Return it immediately!' insisted a vociferous aunt. 'Do they think we cannot keep their daughter until she has all she is used to? She will have to learn to adjust to whatever we can afford, not expect handouts from her parents!'

Gautam meekly carted everything back to Megha's house, explaining to them that although the gesture had been much appreciated, there was simply not enough room in his house for all these items. Then he hurriedly had to refuse the instant offer of an apartment in a nice neighborhood from her father, who was used to exorbitant demands from the families of the other three daughters he had married off.

The rituals began days before the actual wedding.

Gautam's pandit had only contempt for Megha's pandit. 'They don't even have this tilak ceremony! How is he going to conduct the marriage? I had to explain everything to him. But he is so stupid, he won't even remember to bring the auspicious items for the marriage ceremony!'

And when the groom's procession finally arrived at the wedding venue, drums beating and trumpets blaring, a good hour late because of all the dancing on the streets despite Gautam's fervent exhortations, the pandit was proved right. Then a nephew was sent off to fetch the all-important silver supari and yellowed rice. Fortunately, there was enough time to do so while the exchange of garlands took place.

But the real quarrel ensued when the bride, the groom, the bride's parents and the two pandits gathered under the gaily decorated straw roof for the rituals. All the really interested aunts, sisters-in-law and sundry ladies had gathered at the sidelines to comment unfavourably on the opposite side's immediate family and to pass caustic comments on the arrangements or gifts. Barely had the chanting begun when Gautam's pandit claimed it was all wrong, such-and-such ritual had to be completed first, so-and-so invocation made first. Megha's pandit was irked at this doubt over his capabilities. He rose and yelled at his counterpart, who also got to his feet. Both of them got more and more excited while everyone watched aghast. When the two pandits almost came to blows, Gautam's father intervened and quietened down his pandit, who was not supposed to be in charge of this ceremony in the first place. After that, it took a while before Megha's pandit stopped muttering to himself and began the ceremony, scowling intensely at his counterpart every so often.

Gautam still felt the emotion of the moment when Megha's father had placed her hand in his. The sindoor ceremony after that did not affect him as much as the coolness of the small hand resting on his. He had tightened his fingers around hers, hoping she would understand his feelings. She had smiled slightly, her head still bowed.

Later the bride emotionally bid farewell to her family, and the groom's family returned home with their new member. By the time the couple was led into the bridal chamber, tiredness had dulled them. But there were still more rituals to be conducted in the bedroom. A poster had been stuck to the wall painted in red with more auspicious symbols, a comb, the sun, the moon, a kaajal-holder, a palanquin. In earlier times, these would have been painted on the walls, but now a more practical chart paper was used. Vermilion was applied by Megha to all the symbols, the wailing male infant of a cousin was placed on her lap to encourage the birth of sons, it seemed that the entire purpose of marriage was to produce sons; Gautam and she fed each other spoonfuls of kheer.

Finally, with a sense of great achievement as well as great loss, the elderly women conducting the ceremonies reluctantly departed along with the gaggle of young girls who had been enjoying the discomfiture of the groom in the bridal chamber. And so their life together had begun, as had that of countless couples before them, in a cacophony of auspicious incantations, tuneless wedding songs, ancient rituals, fertility symbols, except that unlike many other couples, each knew the other, each could gain strength and support from the other. That made it easier for them to adjust to each other's families.

And then, one day, when he returned from work, his mother told him that Megha had not left her room all day, had not even gone to work. His first reaction was an aching fear that something had happened to her.

'Megha! What's wrong? Are you okay?'

She had turned her head towards him, a frown of concentration on her face and he realized that though she was looking at him, she wasn't really seeing him. Then she shook her head slightly.

Only a mood swing, he was relieved. It would be over soon.

'Would you like some tea? Something to eat?'

Again a single shake of her head. He had stayed with her in the room, talking to her about his day as always. But it wasn't like the other evenings after work when they shared tea and she regaled him with amusing stories from her office.

It took Megha a few days to pull herself out of her depression and she could give him no real reason for it. It just happens, she told him. I feel terrible, miserable, but I can't do anything about it. Sometimes I cry, and I don't know why. I feel as though there is a deep well of sadness inside me. I've been trying and trying for many years to work it all out, to understand myself, reach within and come up with the answer. But I can't, I can't.

He had held her tight then and told her that it didn't matter, that she could have all the moods that she wanted as long as she didn't weep while he was around because that was one thing he wouldn't be able to handle. And she had laughed the laugh he loved and that was the end of it.

Over the years, the inexplicable sadness claimed her every few months and Gautam got used to it, learned to prepare for it, and was there for her even if she didn't really need him. Somehow, he had assumed that when they had children, the problem would resolve itself, but that didn't happen. Through the endless treatments for infertility, Megha became quieter and her entertaining anecdotes about daily events almost ceased. But the periods of darkness did not.

Gautam filed away his memories as his car climbed the neat verdant hills, banked by carefully pruned tea bushes. It passed through tall iron gates and up a flower-bordered driveway and stopped outside a stately building. Narayanan was waiting for him in the office-cum-residence. He greeted Gautam enthusiastically, asked him about his journey, and introduced him to his wife.

'Uma, this is Gautam. He is the fellow whom I keep going to meet in Delhi. Gautam, my wife Uma.'

Uma was a slight figure in a bright sari, long hair coiled up with fragrant flowers, big eyes and a wide smile. 'Namaste, sir,' she smiled at him. 'This is my son, Shankar,' she added, picking up the toddler clinging to her sari.

Gautam, always uncomfortable in the presence of children, reached out to shake the baby's hand, but the child promptly hid his hands behind his back. When Gautam dropped his hand, the baby extended his little grubby hand but when Gautam raised his hand, the baby hid his hands behind his back again. This time, he laughed. It was a game, Gautam realized, and he found himself smiling with the child. An interesting kid, thought Gautam, with his round face and merry eyes, curly hair and toothless smile.

Uma frowned at her son. 'That's enough. Now shake hands properly with the uncle.' She turned to Gautam, 'How old are your children?'

'We don't have any.'

'Oh, newly married, are you?' she looked at him inquisitively, speculatively.

Gautam smiled back casually.

'Show him his room so he can freshen up, Uma. He must be tired after the long journey. We'll have lunch as soon as he is ready.' Narayanan fussed around Gautam, following Uma into another room. The house was a relic of colonial times, with high ceilings, tall pillars, stately rooms. The huge double-bed with its tall teak posts at the corners looked small and insignificant within. 'The bathroom is through that door and there are towels in the cupboard. There is a blanket in this closet if you want to rest after lunch. Here, let me put away your suitcase.'

The child wriggled in his mother's arms to be put down, let out a howl of protest when he wasn't, and started wailing in earnest, limbs going rigid in annoyance at being held tightly. Narayanan took him from his wife's arms.

'Take your time and come when you're ready,' he panted, pretending he didn't have a fidgeting infant in his arms. 'Lunch will be on the table.'

Husband and wife hurried out of the room, trying to calm down the child. Gautam opened his suitcase and went into the bathroom.

During lunch, a maid looked after the baby while Uma and Narayanan joined Gautam at the table. While they ate they talked about the weather, the levels of pollution, the deterioration in civic facilities and other mundane topics. Gautam and Narayanan did most of the talking; Uma was busy watching the child play on the carpet with bright toys while the maid sat on her haunches and stared at nothing.

'Lit-tle doggie, bow-wow,' Uma would suddenly call out. Then, just as abruptly, 'Have more rice, Gautam sir.'

Or, 'Vroom-vroom, up, up in the air goes the plane. Gautam sir came on a plane, Shankar.'

Narayanan said, 'It is because of him that we want to leave this place. It's nice and pleasant but a growing child needs a more cosmopolitan atmosphere where he will get good exposure. We're planning to settle down in Chennai, where Uma's parents live. Would you like to rest a while? We can discuss work in the evening.'

Gautam nodded. Life seemed to slow down here and the pressure he always felt in Delhi was waning under the gentle voice of the mother, the gurgle of the child, and the warmth of the sun. He retired to his room and lay on the high bed and, almost immediately, dropped into a heavy sleep.

It was late and he had to get up, but his eyes would not open. He thought he saw Megha bending over him, and he reached out but she jumped away and laughed, her eyes sparkling, and then he knew he was dreaming because his eyes were still closed and he couldn't have seen hers sparkling. 'Look what I have got,' she laughed and though he couldn't quite see the bundle in her arms, he knew it was her baby, and in his sleep, he was surprised that she had been pregnant and hadn't told him. But the baby was there, swaddled up in the bundle and it was gurgling at him and laughing, and Gautam felt a strange kind of peace sweep over his entire being and he knew that the sound of the baby's laughter was what he had been waiting for a long long time. As the sound continued, he woke up because he realized he was dreaming, a false dream, ephemeral and transient, bringing the kind of fulfilment that was possible only in a dream.

'Sorry to wake you, Gautamji,' said Narayanan, entering the room suddenly, the child in his arms. 'You must have been really tired after the journey. It's almost six now. We will have some tea on the verandah, then we will go into my office.'

'I'll join you in a moment,' said Gautam briskly as he swung his feet down and snapped back to life.

The discussion went well. Narayanan had already made several trips to Delhi to meet with Gautam and his bosses to talk about the preliminary details of the sale. This time, they went over all the charts and agreements and reached the amicable conclusion that they had been heading for right from the start. It was easy to discuss things with Narayanan, Gautam thought, because he didn't let his ego dictate the discussion. Negotiations like these often took much longer simply because the opposite party insisted on certain unreasonable issues merely for the sake of a sense of their own importance.

When everything had been agreed upon, they smiled at each other.

'You'll be sorry to leave this place, I know,' said Gautam. 'How long has it been here?'

'Fourteen years—ever since we got married. I brought Uma here right after our marriage. It's been one long honeymoon for us,' he laughed at his own joke.

'You have a beautiful baby,' Gautam remarked for the sake of saying something nice to Narayanan. He cast about a bit wildly in his mind for a compliment that would make him happy. 'He looks exactly like you, in fact.'

Narayanan chuckled quietly again. 'Do you really think so? He's adopted.'

Gautam felt an inexplicable blow, as if someone had knocked the breath out of him. 'Oh, really?' he blurted out. To hide his shock, he started wrapping up the papers and putting them back in his briefcase. 'I guess I should turn in. I have to make an early start tomorrow.'

The journey back took less time, or so it seemed to Gautam. He felt a lightness of spirit as the car headed down the winding roads towards the plains. He thought it might be due to the fact that he had done what he had come for, but he knew it was more than that. Narayanan had set him on a road towards a solution to what he had never considered a problem. The problem would come now, when he presented his family once again with his wishes, wishes that were by no means the done thing in families like his. But he had got away with it once before and he had been happy. It would solve the problem of Megha's periodic tussles with darkness, he was sure of this with a certainty that surprised him with its strength.

As Gautam made his way back to the guesthouse where he and Megha were staying, he thought of how little Patna had changed since his childhood, when he used to come to visit relatives. It was still chaotic and disorderly, yet the social hierarchies and habits remained as well-defined as ever.

Enquiries about adoption at Delhi had had no progress, with long waiting lists and uncooperative government officials. That was why Gautam was in Patna. But he no longer had relatives here and was out of touch with the people he did know. Pranab bhaiyya seemed sensible and he hoped he would guide him. This afternoon, he was taking Megha to the ancient university town of Nalanda, but he would be back soon and there was plenty of time to meet Pranab bhaiyya later.

7

Pinky's Beautification

PRANAB'S SACRED SATURDAY afternoon nap was rudely interrupted by the unexpected return of Kallu chacha, Chachiji and Pinky.

'Oof!' Kallu chacha exclaimed as soon as Anu opened the door. 'It was such a problem getting an auto to come here. I am exhausted and Chachiji is in great pain. Put lunch on the table quickly so we can eat and then lie down.'

Lunch! Anu had not cooked lunch, having assumed that Kallu chacha and family were gone for the day. There had been enough leftovers from the elaborate breakfast for their own lunch. How was it possible that Kallu chacha had not been offered lunch!

The mystery was soon explained. As Anu put lentils and rice in the pressure cooker and started frying potatoes, Kallu chacha expounded on the advice he had unwillingly received from Chachiji's cousin. It was a long enough story to carry through the preparation of lunch and its consumption.

'Ekdum theek kahat rahey Babua. These days it is important to keep up with changing values. We should have thought of it ourselves, but it is eight years since we married off Guddi, how were we to know that things have changed so much? Those days, boys looked for simple, homely girls. But now, Babua was saying, they want to marry smart girls. He said, look at Pinky, her hair is oiled and tied in two long plaits, and she's not wearing a bit of make-up, who will want such a plain-looking girl. Kay okhra se shaadi karee. I said, So! she should look like a vamp from a TV serial? He said, No, no, but she must wear smart clothes like tight suits and some lipstick-shipstick, otherwise the boy will reject her. I didn't want to sit and listen to more of his nonsense, so I told him I had to meet someone and we left. Except we had to walk a long time in this heat to find a rickshaw that would bring us here. But while sitting in the rickshaw, I discussed it with Chachiji and I realized that really, we must do something about Pinky, she should look a little smarter, not as if she is from some small town. After all, Ranchi is the state capital, badka shahar-va ba-noo, not some backward town. And Pinky is from a proper convent school and knows computers also. The boy will expect her to look like a big town girl. So I told Chachiji she must take her to the beauty parlour and get her hair cut in a good design and also buy her some make-up. It is so expensive getting a daughter married. Betiyan ke biyah khatir ka-ka karey ke padey-la. Of course, she will wear a sari when he comes to see her so it is not necessary to buy a salwar suit, tight or loose. But she says she must rest first, because it was so hot outside.'

After lunch and a nap, Chachiji and Pinky set forth on their important mission with Pranab driving and Radhika as advisor, Chachiji looking sufficiently martyred to attract a pep talk from Kallu chacha who wouldn't accompany them as it was a woman's job. Instead, he had decided to cultivate a cousin of the boy's mother who had been in college with him. Anu stayed back to make dinner for Kallu chacha and the children, and get ready for the birthday party, while Arnab went off to play.

Before he left, Anu asked him to explain the operation of the computer once again.

'Mummy, I have already told you so many times. Why can't you understand? It's not that difficult! I am getting late for my match.'

This was such an exact replica of the words she often used when Arnab had problems with his sums that Anu felt ashamed of her impatience.

Dear Sir,

For a change, I am alone in the house. Kallu chacha got a shock today when he was told by his relative that his daughter was not 'smart'. So he has sent her to a beauty parlour. My husband and daughter went with Pinky and Chachiji, while Kallu chacha decided to go and meet another relative of the boy, hoping to impress him. My son has gone out to play. I have to call my mother to tell her about my talk with my cousin who wants to become a model, and ask about the preparations for the engagement of my other cousin.

I was unable to understand the exact meaning of the circles you mentioned. I am also not too familiar with computers so it is not possible to look at websites. I hope we shall be able to discuss the matter in person when you come.

I met your college friend, Mrs Manvi Prasad, some evenings ago. She is keen to meet you also.

With kind regards,
Anu

She thought she should bring up the topic of Manvi Prasad. What if the professor thought she was out of his life for good and did not expect to meet her during his visit? This would give him time to prepare himself mentally, whether to meet her again or avoid seeing her.

Dear Anu,

I didn't realize you would be such a mine of information! Here I am, carrying out my dry research activities, while you seem to be living at the centre of an action research program specifically designed for my purposes. My field just happens to be cross-cultural psychology and the cultural conceptualization of self-identity.

Since you fit so well into my project, I will need to first interview you. I will be extremely grateful if you would agree to provide me with research material from your own life experiences. You would need to recall incidences pertaining to a certain period, say a week, for this purpose. I hope you will agree to my request.

I am delighted to learn that Mrs Manvi Prasad is keen to meet me. I'd be happy to interview her for the paper. I am not sure I recall being in college with her. Perhaps you can brief me on what aspects to cover when interviewing her. Later, when I am there. Thanks.

Gtg
Girish

Perhaps, Anu concluded, he believed people were not aware of their old romance and did not want to

refer to her. The poor man didn't realize what he was
in for. Many city denizens, the women in particular,
were waiting expectantly at the sidelines of what they
imagined would be a really good drama, better even
than the TV serials, when Girish finally turned up in
town and met Manvi Prasad. The new scandal would
keep the matrons occupied with gossip for a good few
more months. So there was no use to his pretence
that he didn't know Manvi Prasad, thought Anu
sympathetically.

Anu called Amma after she finished cooking dinner.
She still had not been able to tell her about the
conversation with Nanni.

'You shouldn't get too worried, Amma. She hasn't
actually been selected for the advertisement, and even if
she is, the agency appears to be a small one, so even if
they do make the ad, nobody we know will even see it.'

'Boonde-boonde   sagar   bharta   hai,'   said   Amma
dramatically.   'First   she   will   make   this   small
advertisement, then she will be chosen by some big
advertising company, then she will become famous for
selling soap or some fairness cream, then she will become
an important model with her face on billboards all over
the country, and the next thing we know, she will be
appearing in films wearing hardly any clothes at all!'

'If she becomes famous, we will all be proud of her.'

'Nonsense. We will be embarrassed to see her in no
clothes, shaking her hips like a wanton. Have you seen
those horrible songs on MTV? All those gyrating girls
wearing tiny shorts and nothing but bras, throwing
themselves at boys with drooling mouths and groping
hands! So vulgar, so indecent, absolutely disgusting!'

Anu wondered if Amma secretly spent her time watching MTV. She herself often had to prod Radhika or Arnab to switch channels if she saw them watching the hip-grinding Indipop videos.

'I will ask Gunni to speak to her,' Amma continued. 'Gunni will be here this evening, and she can mention it to her uncle who is coming tomorrow. If only Nisha's husband had not passed away so early, she wouldn't have had to face all these problems on her own.'

'She has you to help her.'

'Yes, but it is so difficult for me, because I shouldn't appear to be meddling in someone else's household. That's why I don't say anything to you about giving fruits to the children so that they remain healthy, or about not letting strange men come to your house to stay.'

'He is not a strange man, Amma. Pranab knew him well.'

'But who knows how a person might change after so many years. He has been living in an immoral society where people don't think it wrong to go out with someone else's wife whenever they want to, who knows what sort of morals he has now.'

Anu changed the subject and asked about the preparations for the engagement ceremony. Amma updated her on who was going to fetch the stores and which tentwala had been selected for the canvas covering and the decoration. She herself would be going shopping with Mausi for the gifts that had to be given to the groom's relatives. Anu listened half-heartedly, wondering which other women she could suggest for Girish sir's project until Amma chastised her for not paying attention.

'What is Papa doing?' Anu changed the subject again.

'He has gone to the club to play cards with Devender uncle. I hope they don't return too late. It is not safe driving in the city at night.'

'Amma, I have to go and get my iron from downstairs so that I can get ready.'

'Okay. Call me tomorrow.'

'Okay.'

But Anu didn't go to get ready. There would be plenty of time after Pranab returned with Chachiji and Pinky. Instead, she sat by herself on the sofa and let time pass slowly while it got dark outside.

Why am I not interested in the details of other people's lives? My relationship networks are restricted. I have become too detached. Our scriptures tell us to go beyond earthly desires to find god. But not having earthly desires at all doesn't count, does it?

'Why are you sitting in the dark, Mummy?' asked Arnab when she opened the door for him.

'I was watching how the sun gradually fades away so that we have time to get used to the arrival of darkness each night.'

They sat down on the sofa without switching on the light. Anu put an arm around her sweaty son.

'Why does it get dark so slowly?'

'Because the earth turns away from the sun slowly.'

'What would happen if it turned very fast?'

'Then we would have shorter days and nights and no twilight.'

'Do shadows appear in the twilight?'

'No, there has to be some light for there to be shadows.'

'What would happen if there were no shadows?'

'That would mean that there is only darkness. If even a tiny bit of light exists, there will be shadows. Light and shadows always go together.'

'I wish we could have light and no shadows.'

'Why?'

'I don't like shadows. They are scary.'

'They keep changing, and they look funny, don't they?'

'Yes, and they creep around with me all the time.'

'Well, we just have to get used to them because we can't have one without the other!'

Arnab disengaged himself and jumped up to switch on the light. 'Hello, shadow!' he said, waving a hand at his shadow on the wall. 'Let's dance, shadow,' and he performed a jig that made Anu laugh.

Pinky didn't look very different when she returned from the shopping expedition. Her hair, no longer in tight plaits, had been shampooed and cut till it hung loose just below her shoulders, and Radhika said her eyebrows had been threaded and her face bleached. Still, she just looked a neater version of the old Pinky. But then, a mere visit to the beauty parlour was not enough to smarten up a girl who had been exhorted all her life not to think of herself.

'Now we are going to practise how to do make-up when you and Papa have gone for the dinner,' Radhika declared, looking more excited than Anu had seen her in a while. 'We bought a make-up box with eye shadow and lipstick and blusher and mascara. Look!'

Anu peeped in. The colours in the box looked really garish, but both girls would have a lot of fun playing with them, so she didn't say anything.

'Aren't you ready for Shrivastava's dinner?' Pranab asked, looking rather unhappy about his long outing with two young girls and a complaining Chachiji. Anu noticed the lines of exhaustion around his eyes and felt sorry for him. It had been nice of him to give up his Saturday rest to meet Chachiji's needs.

'Just going,' she called out as she went to her room and she was ready in a few minutes. She didn't bother with anything other than a smear of lipstick and a stroke of kajal. It was going to be an excruciatingly boring evening and Anu saw no reason to dress up just to interact with housewives as dull as her.

As they drove past Gandhi Maidan on their way to Shrivastava's place, Anu asked Pranab for more details about the professor's romance. Gandhi Maidan stretched alongside, a vast expanse of usually green grass unless there was a prolonged dry spell. It was quiet this evening, no crowded exhibitions or political rallies, but on the avenues surrounding it, the city teemed with its usual frenetic activity, vendors pushing carts, buses careening, cars honking.

'He taught her class, I believe. Apparently Manvi used to keep asking him silly questions, but he always responded politely. Some time after the winter break, things got more serious. It seems they were seen together at Bankipore club a few times.'

The ancient club, the bastion of the colonial era, was never very crowded, and at one end, there was a small promenade that looked onto the Ganga, wide and lazy at this point although she still had a long way to go before she reached the sea. The area was not well-lit, either to save electricity costs, or not to disturb the excellent view of the river's undulating expanse. In the days before the new bridge was built, steamers would chug up and down the river, only the constellation of their tiny lights visible in the darkness.

'Then one day, we heard he was leaving. According to Madhu, Manvi was so depressed that she couldn't come to college for several days.'

Before Papa retired, Anu would often spend the long summer vacations with Amma. Often, her sisters would also be there with their children, and the days were spent languorously, chatting, cooking and eating and watching the children play. It was always a reprieve, a vacation, a freedom from responsibilities. Anu had never been so unhappy about being away from Pranab that she became dysfunctional. But then, maybe she was never actually in love.

Shrivastava lived in a small flat in one of the newer colonies. The car bumped precariously over a succession of potholes on the stretch of unpaved road carved out by the construction trucks and left untended since. The exteriors of houses were unplastered and looked like the owners had run out of money before the buildings could be completed. There were few boundary walls and the land was sunk, apparently under the weight of the houses, so low that the monsoon rains would quickly flood the area and make it impassable. Only a decade or so had gone by since this colony had come up and there was little chance of any development in the near future, if at all.

Anu and Pranab climbed the steep unplastered stairs to Shrivastava's second-floor flat where they were among the first to arrive. They entered the hall which was decorated with bright streamers, small balloons and a long shiny cutout that said 'Happy Birthday'. The dining table had streamers all around it and a big cake in the shape of a Mickey Mouse face stared at them cheerfully, a large white candle stuck into its black nose. It all looked very festive and celebratory.

Shrivastava, who worked with Pranab, was from Dhanbad and had made strenuous efforts to get a posting in Patna instead of some small town in Assam. He greeted them at the door and immediately separated husband and wife by taking Pranab to the bedroom. Alcoholic drinks were presumably being served there as the men could not drink in the presence of the old woman who was seated in the main room.

Mrs Shrivastava was short and round. She was wearing a shiny synthetic sari pinned up neatly at the shoulder and had a bold streak of vermilion in her hair. Anu had only met her once before. She sketched a quick namaste to Anu and accepted the red envelope Anu held out to her. Her son, the birthday boy, was decked in an embroidered kurta whose pyjamas were missing as he had already wet them. Fortunately, the kurta was long enough to prevent any embarrassment to the baby.

Mrs Shrivastava invited Anu to sit on a sofa and disappeared into the kitchen. The old woman, skinny and wrinkled, presumably Shrivastava's mother, was comfortably ensconced with her feet up in the armchair to her right and observed the gathering vaguely through thick spectacles. Mrs Dasgupta, the branch manager's wife, had been allotted the place of honour in the centre of the sofa, to Anu's left. Anu greeted her warmly and Mrs Dasgupta graciously inclined her head in response.

Various women whom Anu didn't recognize stood around smiling uncertainly at her, and she presumed they were members of the family but no introductions were made. The hostess remained mostly in the kitchen, emerging only to greet other arriving couples. The baby was carried around by a servant-girl who appeared to be about eight years old. Anu knew that had she asked the age, the servant-girl would be touted as over twelve— after all, Shrivastava's mother would have told her, these poor village children were stunted due to malnutrition, and if they were working, at least they got to eat, so it was actually social service to employ a girl-child as a nursemaid, wasn't it. The girl wore a hand-me-down salwar-kameez that had belonged to Mrs Shrivastava in better times, and the kameez billowed around her slight body and hung down to her feet.

The family members talked among themselves and Anu started a sporadic conversation with the snooty Mrs Dasgupta who appeared to be passing time until it was decent enough for her to leave.

'It has become so hot nowadays,' began Anu.

Mrs Dasgupta graciously inclined her head, turning it a fraction towards Anu.

'It is terrible in the kitchen,' Anu persisted. 'I wonder how poor Mrs Shrivastava has been managing, cooking for such a large gathering.'

'No vegetables available also,' Mrs Dasgupta added graciously.

'Yes, very difficult to find good ones in this in-between season. Where do you buy your vegetables?'

'We do not eat so many vegetables. We eat fish,' Mrs Dasgupta proclaimed.

There was a tap on Anu's shoulder. It was the old woman. 'There are many mines in Dhanbad. The air is black with coal dust,' she informed Anu in a quavering voice, grinding her dentures.

'Ah yes. How long have you been in Patna now?' Anu responded but the old woman had lapsed back into silence. Anu turned back to Mrs Dasgupta.

'Where do you buy fish?'

'At the ghat.'

Mrs Lall, whose husband also worked in the bank, eagerly jumped in to discuss the different varieties of fish available in Kolkata where they had earlier been posted. Anu suspected Mrs Lall had been invited solely because of that posting in Kolkata. Indeed, Mrs Dasgupta was far more amiable and animated now that the conversation ventured into how wonderful a city Kolkata was and how much culture and history it had. Anu desisted from pointing out that it had, until a few hundred years ago, been a small embankment built by the British while Patna was built on the ruins of the greatest city in ancient India, the centre of India's first empire. She remembered a similar conversation at the last party, where Mrs Dasgupta had graciously chided her for living in the past when there was nothing to commend Patna in the present.

As the evening wore on, the women's conversation ranged over the advantages of using Flit over Good Knight to get rid of mosquitoes, the importance of using homemade starch, the various ways to cook fish, the incompetence of child servants, student tutors, the bank which employed most of their husbands, and other topics of general interest. At various times, the old woman would prod Anu in the shoulder and give her some bit of useless information about her hometown or her children. It didn't distract Anu from the main conversation as she wasn't listening in any case.

Arnab needs a tutor now that he is in a higher class. The teachers can't be bothered about individual children, they have to manage sixty students in half an hour. Something needs to be done about the education system. The old woman is saying something I can't understand. Yes, yes, you are right, okay. How can struggling middle-class salaried people afford tutors with so many other obligations to meet? I must get him to sit with me for an hour every day for maths. Numerators, denominators, equivalent fractions...

Anu didn't wonder what the men might be talking about either. Their conversation would always cover a bit of state politics, some criticism of the central government, rumours concerning the amount of money politicians and bureaucrats were making from the various government departments, and then centre on bank politics, transfers, postings and HR policies.

It was after eleven by the time Mrs Shrivastava finished cooking and emerged from the kitchen, looking rather dishevelled, holding a vegetable knife decorated with a bright streamer. The men were summoned from the bedroom, Shrivastava brought out his camera, the infant was roused from his nap on the divan, the little girl-servant was shaken awake from where she had curled up to sleep on the floor, the family members gathered around the table, and Mrs Shrivastava held the wailing baby and cut the cake to a round of applause from all present. The happy birthday song was rendered loudly but tunelessly by the more drink-afflicted gentlemen, who then wanted Mrs Shrivastava to feed her husband with a piece of cake on behalf of the baby. She gave an embarrassed smile, handed the crying baby to the servant girl and started setting the food on the table with the help of her family members.

Fish was naturally included as well as chicken, paneer, chhole and various sabzis, along with pulao and puris. Everyone exclaimed at the trouble Mrs Shrivastava had taken and set to with gusto. It didn't take too long to dispose of the food, but this was followed by Mr Dasgupta's insistence on regaling them with stories about his days as a young probationer until Mrs Dasgupta made a light remark about boring the gathering. The gathering laughed dutifully, but Mrs Dasgupta prevailed and at last the dinner broke up. Everyone followed the Dasguptas down the unlit uneven staircase, waited until they had driven off, then got into their own cars and began the long drive home.

'That was a nice party,' Pranab remarked but Anu didn't respond.

Everyone was still up when Anuradha and Pranab reached home and Kallu chacha was in an uncharacteristic state of agitation.

'I couldn't even watch the movie tonight,' he lamented, 'even though it was such an interesting romance with so many good songs. Tabah-tabah ho gaeeni! This Arun told me that the boy's father is arriving tomorrow morning itself. Even the boy is coming. There are two other girls they are planning to see, so they are coming early. I wonder if my letter about Pinky didn't reach him because he did not reply to it although I sent the horoscope and even the photo. Now I will have to hurry up and meet him tomorrow before he meets the fathers of the other two girls. Arun told me that the girl and the family are the only consideration and they want milky-white complexion.'

Everyone looked at Pinky to see how far her complexion could be stretched to come under that exalted category. Maybe wheatish would have been a better description for her.

'I will come with you,' Pranab offered. 'Where will they be staying?'

'At Gyani babu's house in Rajendra Nagar. The whole engagement party is staying on the newly built second floor.'

Sombrely, the family brought out the mattresses, moved the centre table, spread out the sheets and pillows, and got ready for bed, overcome with the prospect of disaster.

'Why did you have to offer to go?' Anu confronted Pranab later in the privacy of their room.

'The poor man has been trying so hard to find a match for the girl. I felt obliged to help him.'

'Emotional blackmail,' muttered Anu, escaping into the bathroom before Pranab could retaliate.

Interlude

The haat was held every Thursday in the adjoining
village, a raucous colourful conglomeration of stalls,
pushcarts and sheets on the ground, selling everything
a household could possibly need. On the appointed
day, Srijana Devi woke before dawn and made sure all
her tasks were completed in time. She prodded awake
Kishna, her daughter, and they walked to the fields
together. Bantu and Chintu still slept, limbs entangled
on the chowki in the open space in front of the hut.
On their way back from the field, Srijana and Kishna
collected bits of wood, leaves and cow-dung. By the time
they reached home, the sun was already hot. It seemed
to take longer to light the fire and even longer to cook
the rice.

After her husband left to look for the day's work in
the city, Srijana fed her children and then ate herself.
She had already told the other women she would not
be going with them to work in the fields and those of
them who knew the importance of the day had eyed her
enviously.

Gauri didi drove up in a battered old car around noon.
Srijana knew this was not the right time to go to the
haat because the traders would start with the highest
prices at the beginning of the day. It was only after
sundown, when the crowds started thinning, that prices
would come down as the traders became desperate to
sell their remaining ware. But she was too excited about
going to the haat to mention these minor details to Gauri

didi. Besides, surely it was better to go early when the healthiest goats were available. After all, a goat was not a vegetable or a piece of fish that had to be sold perforce by the end of the day.

In keeping with the importance of the occasion, Srijana dressed festively in her brightest yellow sari with a bindi and 'gold' earrings, her hair oiled and tied neatly at the back. Seeing their mother about to sit in a car, Bantu, Chintu and Kishna clamoured to accompany her. Gauri didi laughed and agreed to take them along, pleased with the children's excitement at something as simple as a car.

They bundled into the car, Bantu and Chintu sitting in front to examine the knobs and dials of the dashboard. The road was bumpy and as they approached the haat, it became increasingly crowded as men, women and children in their best clothes walked or cycled to the venue. Finally, they turned off onto a dusty track that led to the maidan.

The maidan was a melee of hectic activity as traders laid out their wares, rows of colourful glass bangles, bright polyester saris in all hues, t-shirts and scarves, piles of eatables on hand-carts, neat lines of shining steel utensils, plastic buckets, mugs, containers, cheap painted toys of weak metals and plastic, cars, buses, dolls, guns, flimsy bits of wooden furniture, and at the end, next to the chicken coops, the small enclosure packed with bleating goats.

Srijana could see Gauri didi looking at her watch as she ran the car round a mound and switched it off. It was immediately surrounded by a crowd of chattering boys who pushed each other to get a closer look at the occupants. There were other cars parked nearby, including one with the official red light on top and a few police jeeps. But there was no sign of any constables or officials trying to maintain order.

Gauri didi was already in a hurry to leave. The journey had taken longer than she had expected and the excitement of the boys in the car had worn down her enthusiasm for the expedition. She was going to get Srijana to buy the first goat she saw, pile it into the car, and ferry them all back to their hut as soon as possible. Besides, it wasn't safe to spend too long at these kinds of places. Who knew when a dangerous altercation would break out or some thugs would descend to make easy money? In Bihar, anything was possible at any time and it was best to keep oneself out of the line of fire.

She had not bargained for the time it would take to reach the goat enclosure. One or the other of the kids kept running off, Srijana kept stopping at the stalls, and Gauri didi often found herself abandoned in the centre of the milling crowd, frantically waving to her group to gather again. By the time they reached the goats, she was very irritated and seriously thinking of abandoning her entire venture into grassroots micro-credit. Srijana's was only one of twenty-three women's self-help groups in the area under her supervision, and the lack of initiative and enthusiasm from the 'target beneficiaries' was a source of great frustration. These women did not seem interested in their economic upliftment, being mired in their traditions, and one goat more or less was not going to move them up any income ladders.

But when they reached the goat-pen she was surprised at the knowledge and bargaining skills Srijana displayed. She found herself watching keenly as this underprivileged, illiterate woman efficiently moved among the goats, identified the one she wanted and haggled vociferously with an equally vocal trader on the price. Finally, the deal was concluded with the trader muttering to himself as he tied a string to the goat which he handed to a beatifically smiling Srijana.

The kids exclaimed over the frisky black goat, stroking its back and fondling its ears. Srijana Devi continued to smile ecstatically, her eyes shining with the promise of the future. She looked beautiful.

Well, decided Gauri didi, perhaps field work was not so bad after all.

8

Sunday

AMMA CALLED EARLY in the morning. 'I have asked Gunni, Nanni and Nishu for lunch. Their uncle Munna is also coming. His family couldn't come for the engagement because his daughter had exams. You must come for lunch too.'

'Kallu chacha is going to meet the boy's father. Chachiji and Pinky will be here,' Anu informed her.

'I have made arrangements for them. You know Sudha, who lives in the next block, she was telling me the other day that someone has occupied her village land near Ranchi. So I told her Kallu would be a good person to ask for advice. I called her today and she wants him to come for lunch. Give him the message.'

'Dekhatani. If I am free by lunchtime, I will go,' Kallu chacha agreed in a long-suffering tone. He couldn't resist adding that with his daughter's marriage looming over his head, he could hardly be expected to think about other people's land problems.

'Chachiji and Pinky can come in our car as it is close to Amma's house,' Anu clarified hastily, and so it was decided.

Kallu chacha had already asked a friend to take him to meet the boy's father that morning. When the friend presented himself in his new Alto, Pranab was still not ready, and Kallu chacha, unwilling to wait for him, set off immediately, armed with copies of Pinky's biodata, horoscope and photograph.

After breakfast, Anu sat with Arnab and the mathematics textbook, but her thoughts kept straying to the professor's careless remark about not remembering Manvi Prasad. It had bothered her the whole night. Was love ultimately so ephemeral? Setting Arnab some exercises, she went to her e-mail.

Dear Sir,

I am trying to follow your instructions to note down my life over this week. It has been a very busy time, with Kallu chacha's mad rush to get Pinky married, Gunni's engagement preparations, the maid's family problems, Amma's schemes to prevent Nanni from becoming a model, etc. Now that I am making notes, I find there is quite a lot happening around me. Only, I don't feel involved. It's as if I am a spectator to my own life. For example, yesterday evening, we went to a birthday party for a child, where everyone was chatting animatedly about mosquito control and fish recipes and I just couldn't be part of the conversation. Perhaps I was tired.

Mrs Manvi Prasad was a student in your sociology class. She was a classmate of Madhu's, Pranab's younger sister. Her father was in the police service. She married an IPS officer and is now a lecturer in a local college. Her

children are in Delhi. She remembers you very fondly. I
hope you will meet her.

Looking forward to your arrival,
Anu

The reply was almost immediate.

Dear Anu,

Thank you very much for helping me out with this project.
It means a lot to me.

Don't worry so much about being different from other
people. We can't all be a part of every community. Some
of us are misfits wherever we are. Neither society nor
we can hold ourselves accountable for these occasional
mismatches. If society were one vast homogenous whole,
where every person was just another cog in the wheel,
there would be no creativity and innovation, no art, no
inventions, no progress. Some of us are lucky enough that
we can express ourselves.

Now that you mention it, I do remember a student
who may have been Manvi Prasad. It will be interesting to
catch up with her.

I am frantically trying to wind up a lot of matters
before I catch my flight, but I'm afraid that most things
will be just left half done!

See you soon.
Girish.

And for the time being, Anu had to be content with
that.

Gunni, Nanni and Nishu mausi were already at
Amma's flat by the time Pranab's red Maruti trundled
up to the block of flats. Munna chacha, the girls'

uncle, was also there. He was a tall and cheerful man, full of bonhomie and good spirit, and had an excellent relationship with his nieces, who had been under his guidance for many years.

Amma's flat, on the first floor of a private builder's block, was rather crowded as the household effects of sprawling bungalows in small towns had to be squeezed into the three-bedroom accommodation after Papa retired. But as Amma often pointed out, she wasn't complaining that her husband had not had the foresight to purchase a plot of land in the days when they had been available at ridiculously low prices. After all, they had had three daughters to marry off and all their resources had been conserved for that purpose only. And hadn't her continuous thrift, she added, ensured the success of this objective?

'Kya hua?' Amma greeted them. 'How come you're so late?'

'Golu had to study for his maths test and then we had to drop off Chachiji and Pinky,' Anu explained. 'Pranam, Munna chacha, when did you arrive?'

Munna, only a year or two senior to Pranab at college, graciously bestowed his blessings on Anu, and said, 'Just this morning. I thought there would be a lot of work to be done before Wednesday, so I came early. Hello, Nabbu, I believe you will have an interesting visitor this week.'

'Yes, my old professor, Girish Chandra Verma. Did you also study under him?'

'No, but I visited him occasionally with my friends. What interesting discussions we had about the world! He gave me some good books to read.'

Nanni brought orange soda on a tray just then. Pranab looked a little surprised at her appearance but didn't say anything. Today, she was wearing black pants with studs along the sides and a white lacy blouse through which a velvet chemise was very visible. With her high heels, she topped Pranab by a formidable two inches, though she was still shorter than her uncle.

Nisha mausi was sitting on the sofa with Gunni. After Anu had greeted them they listened to the men talk about Girish sir. Apparently, he had once got into a huge argument with the university vice-chancellor and the head of department because they insisted that only topics within the syllabus be covered in class. Then the scandal involving Manvi Prasad was rehashed, quite vaguely as nobody seemed to know the details. Anu listened with avid interest, occasionally asking questions about the major romance that had been the talk of the town twenty years ago.

'I heard he left in such a hurry that he had no job or money when he reached America. Someone told me he was forced to work as a janitor for several months while applying for the position of lecturer,' said Munna.

'Did he? But he should have completed his PhD before applying for a job.'

'Maybe he did that first. Maybe that's why he was a janitor. In America, anyone can be a janitor and clean floors and bathrooms to earn money. Not like India. But it will be really interesting to meet him when he comes here. Bring him for the engagement when you come; what will he do alone at home? I wonder if Manvi Prasad knows he is coming.'

'Everyone in Patna knows by now,' Anu interjected but was ignored.

'He really was an outstanding teacher,' said Pranab. 'And such a riveting speaker! Sadly, there is no incentive in our system for such people to stay if there are better opportunities.'

Papa came in, having gone to the shop nearby for ice-cream. Gunni got up to take it from him but Amma came out from the kitchen and took it herself, saying, 'No, no, Gunni, I'll put it away.'

Gunni laughed, 'Mausiji, you haven't let me get up from the sofa at all today!'

'Why should you get up when you are to be engaged in two days' time? You have to rest to look good. Besides, Nanni hai na.' The ice-cream brick was promptly handed to Nanni who carried it back to the kitchen along with the empty glasses.

Amma made Nanni run around all afternoon, laying the table, serving the food, serving the ice-cream and other such mundane tasks designed to bring her down to earth and reiterate the reality that she was not a glamorous model but a middle-class girl who had to prepare for married life. After lunch was over and Nanni was clearing away the dishes, Amma finally turned to Munna chacha.

'Ever since you have been posted out of Delhi, there has been no one to look after Nanni in the hostel,' she began. 'There is no one to guide and advise her.'

Gunni laughed. 'But Mausiji, I am there now, have you forgotten?'

'You are an immature girl yourself. And your work keeps you very busy, I'm sure. The girl needs a capable person to know what she is doing and tell her if it is correct or not.'

Munna chacha said, 'Didi, I am sure Nanni is doing very well in her studies. She is a responsible girl.'

'Studies aren't everything, Munna. Did you know she wants to become a model?'

'She did mention something,' was his vague reply as he suddenly realized that he had been derelict in his duties as self-appointed guardian even if he was no longer in the same city as Nanni.

Amma pounced on him righteously. 'Zara socho! I am sure you yourself know what a disaster it would be for the girl to go into such an immodest profession. Log kya kahenge? Think of the scandal your family will have to face; think of your daughter. It won't be good for her either if Nanni is allowed to do what she plans.'

Nanni came up. 'Mausiji, it's not that bad. These days, everyone is trying to enter this glamorous field. Why can't I?'

'Chup! Don't talk nonsense. You are just a young girl, you don't realize the meaning or consequences of what you are saying. I know there are many mothers in big cities who push their ugly daughters to join films or modelling or music contests. But we in Patna are not like that. Okay, maybe some are, but people from our kind of families cannot accept it. Munna, see what ideas she has got after going to the hostel? I told you it would not be proper if you took a transfer from Delhi.'

'It was not my choice,' mumbled Munna chacha feebly.

'I will speak to Nanni, Mausiji,' interjected Gunni, while Nanni retreated from the view of her irate aunt. 'She will concentrate on her studies and not think of these stupid ideas.'

'But Didi…!' Nanni protested indignantly. She stopped at a conspiratorial look in her sister's face and said no more.

How clever of Gunni! I wish I could manage Amma's bits of advice as tactfully as that. Amma would have further pushed her point, but suddenly Kallu chacha burst in through the open door, Chachiji and Pinky in tow.

'Tomorrow! They will see the girl tomorrow!' he announced dramatically.

Cries of how and when and where greeted this statement.

'I met the father and just as I had thought, he had not received my letter at all. Ka bhaeel? Otherwise, I thought, how could he not respond to such a good match? The girl is educated and has an almost-white complexion and the family is so well established, Nabbu in the bank, Guddi married to an engineer, Shambhu well settled. And I also told him about Talluji and Gobindji and Abhay Kumar Sinha. He said the boy would decide himself after seeing the girl but I could see he was impressed. So I said, what better day than tomorrow. So he will come at four to our house… he, his cousin, the cousin's wife and two children—I said bring the children also—and the boy himself! I saw him there. He's so handsome. I told Pinky, you like Aamir Khan, this boy looks just like him! It will be a good match.'

'Why are you giving the girl false hopes?' said Amma mildly. 'She has been seen before, she knows how it is.'

'This is different. Jaldi-jaldi chalal jayee! A lot has to be done before tomorrow.'

The party broke up, the children were summoned from the front of the TV and everyone headed down the stairs, Amma rolling her eyes at Anu to convey her sympathy. But Anu was not really upset. She might now get an opportunity to go to the market after all.

Kallu chacha talked most of the way home. As it was Sunday, the roads were marginally less congested. The car, however, was quite congested, and the journey seemed longer than usual. Chachiji took up most of the back seat so Radhika sat on Pinky's lap, while Arnab was squashed between Kallu chacha and Pranab in the front. The plan, as delineated by Kallu chacha in great detail, was to capitalize on the impression he had already made on the boy's father. Having gone through this process several times in the past with no success, he was planning to change his tactics somewhat. On earlier occasions, there had been little emphasis on the food and tea provided—samosas, rasgullas and a salty 'mixture' being deemed adequate—but with a match as important as a doctor, due care would have to be taken of the culinary aspect. He dismissed Anu's cooking as not up to the required standard, which was a big relief for her, and decided to opt for snacks from Cozy Sweets. That meant someone would have to drive across town to fetch them; in the meaningful pause that followed, Pranab was compelled to volunteer. There was unfortunately no time to get the drawing room painted or get the curtains washed, and did Pranab have to hang up his wife's ancient paintings on the walls? How much brighter some nice cheerful framed posters would look, the one of the two English babies, or of the English countryside with a moral message in elaborate lettering.

At this point, Anu mentioned that she was planning to buy new cushion covers, antimacassars and a tablecloth, so she could go in the afternoon to the market. Radhika reminded her that it was Sunday and most of the shops would be closed. Anu groaned inwardly. No matter, said Kallu chacha, at least the covers could be washed in time for the momentous occasion. Pinky would also have to prepare by applying haldi and besan on her face to make it look brighter and perhaps even improve her complexion somewhat. So much had to be done, but thankfully he had thought of everything and Anu and Pranab could manage the rest.

The rest of the evening was a mad rush.

9

Monday

THE NEXT DAY was no better. The activity started as soon as the children left for school. Pranab's departure for work was barely noticed. Since he planned to take the afternoon off, there was no need to pack his lunch.

Every couple of hours, Chachiji would apply the haldi, besan and cream mixture on Pinky's face, trying to make up for all the years she had neglected to do so. Anu had to wash the cushion covers, tablecloths and antimacassars, a task she tackled by dumping them in soapy water, swirling them around a bit, then rinsing them. Fortunately, Chachiji was too busy with Pinky to notice.

The maid was tempted with the promise of a few extra rupees to sweep the corners, get rid of cobwebs and dust the sofa and curtains vigorously to shake off the accumulated dirt of many months. Once she realized the purpose of all this extra work, the maid was enthusiastic enough; after all, it wasn't every day that a boy came to see the girl and she knew the importance of making an impression on the groom's father. Besides, she needed the extra money herself as the engagement of her daughter had been fixed a second time for the following Sunday and she would have to buy five chickens again, as the last lot had been wasted when the irate prospective mother-in-law departed without concluding the ceremony.

The maid took keen interest in the proposed match, and between beating the durrie with a rod, running over the furniture with a damp cloth and poking a broom tied to a pole into the ceiling corners, she managed to gather a fair amount of background information from Chachiji who was following her around to make sure she was doing a decent job. Exchanging notes on boys, ceremonies, the problems of having daughters and other such topics of mutual interest, Chachiji and the maid spent an agreeable and useful morning together.

The presswala made a face when he saw the pile of cushion covers, tablecloths and antimacassars, but agreed to do them quickly after he had heard the reason and haggled on a satisfactory rate for these unusual items. 'Taking advantage of our urgency!' snorted Chachiji. Anita from downstairs, who tried to hang around to get more details of the coming event, was also packed off firmly by Chachiji who was in her element today.

The selection of the sari from Anu's cupboard was a long affair. The dark saris had to be rejected because they reflected shadows on the girl's skin and the pastel-coloured saris might make her look dark in comparison. The organdie saris would make her look fat but the cotton ones would get crushed easily and appear untidy. The nylon saris could not be considered formal wear at

all but the silk saris would not appear casual enough.
After holding up several saris against Pinky and berating
Anu for not having any new saris at hand, Chachiji
finally unearthed a peacock-blue silk with a Rajasthani
print which had done the rounds as a gift several times
before Anu received it. She had worn it only a couple
of times in the past few years as she felt the colour was
much too bright. However, it was quite suitable for the
much younger Pinky and since there weren't any proper
alternatives, they were compelled to use it, even though
it was silk.

Kallu chacha, who had gone out to obtain relevant
information from a friend, came home for lunch and
was pleased with the arrangements so far. 'Yes, at least
the cushions are almost like new now. Sab theekay ba.
Table-va door ba, so nobody will notice the stains on the
plastic tablecloth. We will serve the snacks here itself,
no need to spread them out on the table. Bring all the
chairs from the dining table here, Golu. Pinky can sit on
a chair there, near the window so that the light falls on
her face. Radhika can come in with her since Anu will
be busy with the food. And we must keep the TV on for
the children. The boy and his father can sit on the sofa.'

After a late lunch, Pranab left immediately to fetch the
snacks from Cozy Sweets. Arnab and Radhika, for once,
behaved responsibly, choosing their own clothes for the
event and making themselves presentable.

There was no time to check her e-mail.

Four p.m. being the appointed hour, everyone was
ready and waiting except Pranab, who had still not
returned from Cozy Sweets. Kallu chacha was not
worried, though. 'He must be waiting there so that

the snacks are still hot when they get here,' he said reassuringly, but Anu was very anxious. She called Pranab surreptitiously from the kitchen to ask him if she should prepare something in case he was held up in traffic, but he told her he would be back before the important guests arrived.

Pinky was carefully dressed in the blue sari and had liberally applied face powder, blusher and lipstick from the new make-up box. Fortunately, Anu had checked in on her and Radhika, and wiped most of it off. She had also insisted that Pinky's hair not be left wild to stream around her shoulders since, unlike the models in shampoo commercials, Pinky's hair tended to be frizzy rather than smooth. A compromise was achieved and her hair was tied loosely at the back, leaving enough tendrils to frame her face. Radhika decided to leave her own hair open in order to impress on the visitors that the family was actually quite modern. Kallu chacha had made Pinky sit by the window and proclaimed her 'fair enough'. Now she was waiting in the bedroom with Radhika.

Arnab, who had been keeping watch from the balcony, excitedly announced the arrival of the guests at half past four. By the time they had climbed the stairs and appeared huffing and puffing at the door, the whole family was lined up at the entrance to receive them, except Pinky who was to remain in her room.

'Aaiye-aaiye, welcome, welcome!' Kallu chacha greeted them, for once dispensing with his favorite Bhojpuri. 'This is the girl's mother, and the girl's Bhabhi, and this is Arnab, and Radhika. Please have a seat, please sit down.'

There were namastes all around, everyone smiling politely. The boy's father was a tiny bespectacled man, dyed black hair ringing a bald pate. His cousin was much younger, short and paunchy with thick grey hair and a moustache to match. His wife, also short and round, was dressed in a printed bright orange polyester sari. Their two sons were also pudgy, a little younger than Arnab, and wore matching baba suits. The boy entered last, and despite their curiosity, the hosts studiously avoided inspecting him as it would be considered improper. He was taller than his father, slim, quite dark-skinned, also bespectacled and beginning to go bald at the edges. Not at all like Aamir Khan. Radhika slipped out of the room to report to Pinky.

Arnab led the two boys to the chairs right in front of the TV and the adults were carefully manoeuvred by Kallu chacha into their designated seats. Anu hurried into the kitchen to fetch the mandatory glasses of water. But where was Pranab?

'It has become so hot now,' Kallu chacha began. 'How is Arrah?'

'Arrah is very hot too,' replied Mr Sahay, the boy's father. 'Last winter was very cold, so the summer is bound to be very hot.'

'Arre nahi, Sahay saab. If the winter is cold, the summer is mild.'

'Oh no. My mother always said that a cold winter means unusually hot summers, and also heavy rain during the monsoons.'

'In Ranchi, if the winters are very cold, the summers are always mild. And, of course, the rains...'

'And where are you from?' Chachiji interrupted loudly, turning to the cousin's wife.

The young woman smiled at Chachiji, then looked towards her husband for guidance. He replied for her, 'My wife is from Buxar, from the family of Lal Behari Sinha, the one whose cousin is the MLA.'

'Oh, I know their family very well,' said Kallu chacha. 'Their younger son's son-in-law used to live across the street from us when we lived in Ashok Nagar. I don't know where he has gone after his transfer. He was with the coal department. Do you know where he is now?'

'I think he has gone to Raipur on deputation. But the other son-in-law is in Buxar.'

'Yes, I remember the younger son had four daughters. And all that property in the family,' Kallu chacha clicked his tongue and shook his head.

'The sons-in-law are enjoying the property, they sell it whenever they need money, and they get rice, dal, oil, all from the farms.'

With major effort, Kallu chacha refrained from passing judgement on the greed of sons-in-law and the importance of having sons, and asked if the guests would prefer colas or nimbu-pani. The two little boys opted for Coke and the adults decided to have the same. Nobody would want home-made nimbu-pani when there was Coke.

Anu picked up the glasses and went into the kitchen. Where was Pranab! She washed and wiped the glasses, poured Coke into them from the two-litre bottle, arranged them on the tray and took them out to the drawing room, trying to do everything very slowly, hoping that Pranab would turn up. The conversation flickered from one topic to another, with Kallu chacha trying to drop as many names of his important relatives and friends as possible. The boys had decided to watch cartoons, which helped bridge the awkward moments. Then Chachiji decided that instead of waiting for the snacks, they could move on to the viewing of the girl.

She waddled up to the bedroom and instructed Pinky and Radhika to come to the living room. She hissed a few last-minute instructions. 'Keep your head low. Don't smile. Look serious.'

But Pinky was a veteran of such inspections and knew exactly how to conduct herself. She minced her way into the drawing room, her head lowered at the precise angle that would denote shy confidence. She was followed by Radhika, excited at having graduated from mute spectator to centre stage.

Pinky sat carefully at the edge of her appointed seat with Radhika hovering protectively behind her. Kallu chacha made an indistinct remark introducing her as 'my daughter, Anahita', then everyone ignored her. After a few more minutes of desultory conversation about road conditions in Bihar, Chachiji gestured to the cousin's wife to sit next to Pinky.

The cousin's wife looked enquiringly at her husband, and he giggled nervously and mumbled something, gesticulating at the boy.

Kallu chacha and Chachiji were speechless. Was the cousin actually implying that the boy wanted to speak to the girl himself? This was simply not done in respectable families. But then, Kallu chacha seemed to catch up with the times in the space of a single moment. With obvious reluctance, he made half a gesture of agreement.

The cousin giggled nervously again and said, 'No, he wants to meet the girl alone.'

This was too much even for the newly modernized Kallu chacha. He opened his mouth, but before he could expound on the dignity of his old and reputed family, Chachiji said, 'We must become modern now, ji. Let them go to the bedroom with Radhika. We can watch from here.'

Pinky shuffled back to the bedroom, followed by the boy and Radhika. They sat down on the edge of the bed. The gathered party strained its collective ears but couldn't catch even a fragment of the low conversation that was conducted between the boy and the girl.

After a moment, Mr Sahay started talking about how well his son was doing in his practice, how dedicated he was to social causes and how he chose to treat poor patients for next to nothing. This generosity weighed heavily on the minds of his parents as it considerably reduced the son's income, but what to do, they had to bear with having a socially conscious son. Kallu chacha listened with increasing trepidation. He had been led to believe that dowry was not an issue. But ultimately, could a doctor be separated from his dowry?

'I can understand your problem, Sahay saab. Living expenses have gone up so much, and nowadays, young people want to have a car and a cellphone and other things that were not there in our youth. And who are we to deprive them? I myself, being a retired person, feel so bad when I am not able to buy things for Pinky. But my money has gone towards my children's education. That is the most important thing we parents can give our children after all.'

'You are right, Verma saab. I too, had to take a loan for my son's education, especially when he wanted to go to the UK to study. We still haven't been able to repay the loan despite scrimping and saving every rupee. Fortunately, my daughters are already married. We had to give each of our sons-in-law a car as well as money.'

At that point, Pranab entered with big plastic bags. 'Ah!' exclaimed Kallu chacha in double relief. 'Sahay saab, my nephew, Pranab Verma. I told you about him. He is a bank manager.'

Things were easier after that. Anu took control of the food and Pranab of the conversation. The snacks were served and the boy was summoned back into the living room. Pinky and Radhika were given their plates in the bedroom. Everyone ate enthusiastically, and the guests seemed happy with the cutlets, kachoris and milk sweets. Kallu chacha piled them with more and more, 'Leejiye-leejiye na!' until they were satiated and resisted further exhortations. By the time tea was served, many common friends and relatives had been unearthed and a genuine bonhomie established between the exalted guests and their hosts. At last, the guests said their goodbyes and everyone clattered down the stairs to see them off.

'What did you talk about?' Pinky was quizzed when they returned. She wouldn't say, but Radhika gave a full account of the conversation.

'He asked her where she had studied, and what she liked doing. He asked how she had done in her college exams and computer course. Then he asked her what movies she liked. He also asked what she thought of dowry.'

'Dowry! What did she say?'

'She said it was not a good practice. So he asked why, and she said that parents have to spend on educating their daughters as much as they do on their sons. Then he said he didn't like dowry because he felt it was like the boy is being sold! And they both laughed.'

'Laughed!' lamented Kallu chacha. 'Now he will think Pinky is not a serious-minded girl!'

'No, no, Dadaji, he was very happy, I could tell. He liked her a lot.'

'That doesn't matter. It means nothing if he likes her or not, or if he wants dowry or not. It all depends on his father and mother. I will call them tomorrow morning and see what they say.'

Pranab had bought extra kachoris, cutlets and milk cakes, fearing that they might fall short. So Anu didn't have to do any cooking for dinner, apart from making parathas. She listened from the kitchen to Pranab's and Kallu chacha's analysis of the conversations between Sahay saab and Kallu chacha, between Pranab and the boy, between the boy and Pinky, trying to figure out their chances.

As if this dissection will help decide the issue! After dinner, the TV was switched on, but nobody paid much attention to the serials as there was a gloomy atmosphere of suspense and tension over the visit.

And then there was a miracle.

During a commercial break, there was a phone call for Kallu chacha. 'Sahay saab! Oh! No, no, no problem... yes, yes... no, no... okay, okay... yes, yes... namaste.'

He put down the phone and sat down on the nearest chair.

'Any news?' Pranab asked gently.

Kallu chacha seemed breathless. 'He said he wanted to meet me tomorrow,' he gasped. 'Before Gunni's

engagement party. He asked if we were ready to do
the engagement soon. Then he said we will discuss it
tomorrow.'

Pranab smiled delightedly. 'That means they have
agreed! The marriage is fixed!'

Kallu chacha said, 'No, he has not yet said anything
definite. We still have to discuss tomorrow. We will
know for sure only tomorrow. Who knows what may
happen between today and tomorrow? He has not given
his word yet.'

Arnab broke out into a dance. 'Pinky bua is getting
married, Pinky bua is getting married!' he chanted, until
Anu shushed him.

'Now we can look for a girl for Shambhu also,'
mumbled Chachiji, but very softly in case there was no
positive word the next day.

Interlude

Srijana may not have looked after her children as well as she cared for the goat. She knew the art of goat-keeping since she had tended to the animals of the landlord, who spent far more time and energy on his mute flock than on his tenants and employees. A vet was summoned regularly for the animals. The best grains with added nutrients were provided lovingly and fed under his personal supervision. Their enclosures were regularly cleaned and sanitized. Indeed, the landlord's animals lived in far better condition than many humans.

But now Srijana could understand his concerns. One paid money for an animal. If it died due to poor care, it took not only the investment but also the future profits. This was her own goat, which she had earned after months of saving, months of attending the self-help group meetings, months of longing, and she was going to care for it under all circumstances!

The other members of the group displayed extraordinary envy, which in itself was a matter of great satisfaction. Srijana received many visitors who just came to stare at her goat as if to convince themselves that joining a self-help group was a profitable activity. Many skeptics, doubting the benefits of saving ten rupees a month towards their future, came with queries and left with promises to join, while those who were members just turned up to pass idle time and hope for their own future. Srijana felt quite important after all these visits.

Gauri didi also came once in a while to look up Srijana. The other woman who had been selected for the small loan had decided to sell vegetables and was already making tiny but encouraging profits. Every week, she returned a fraction of the loan and Gauri didi was very pleased with the 'demonstration effect' that the loan had initiated. The response from the 'target group' had increased substantially after the vegetable seller had repaid the money borrowed from the village loan shark shortly after starting her business.

Srijana would repay the group's loan when the goat was ready to be sold a few months later. In the meantime, Gauri didi wanted to make sure that nothing happened to the goat which might lower the current level of interest of the village women in the programme. If the animal fell sick and died, that would be the end of her project here. A lot rode on the well-being of the creature.

Right now, the goat, barely more than a kid really, was active and frisky. Even tethered, it remained on its toes and seemed excited when approached by humans. Sometimes, when one or the other of the children untied it, it raced around, making them run after it with the rope.

What a pity its destiny was to add to someone's table!

10

Tuesday

KALLU CHACHA COULD barely wait for the children to vacate the bathroom so he could get ready for the important meeting. It might have been early but he still needed to be dressed in order to think in peace about what he wanted to say to Sahay saab. While he waited for Radhika to emerge from the bathroom, Chachiji gently reminded him that there was no point in thinking too much about it as he would have to accept whatever the boy's family demanded. But he insisted that negotiations were all a matter of strategy. Even grooms' families, he informed her, could be persuaded with a little tact and subtlety which needed advance planning. Having worked his whole life in an office, Kallu chacha was not used to strategic thinking until he was properly dressed and breakfasted as Chachiji well knew, so she should ask Radhika to hurry up instead of saying irrelevant things and distracting him.

Kallu chacha couldn't wait for Pranab to get ready for office in his usual unhurried manner either, so after gulping down a bowlful of leftover chapattis and bananas crushed into milk, he rushed out and was seen hopping urgently into a passing rickshaw.

Girish Chandra Verma would arrive in a couple of days. Anu was no longer worried about what she needed to buy for him. There was little chance of her going anywhere while Kallu chacha was around, she had finally realized. Besides, the flat looked a little better after the frenetic cleaning it had received at the hands of the maid the previous day. And in any case, after spending a night in the same room as Kallu chacha, the professor would probably be desperate enough to find another place to stay the very next day.

The phone rang while Pranab was having breakfast. It was Amma with bad news. Mira di's mother-in-law had passed away suddenly.

'The cremation is in the afternoon. Nobody knows what happened. She had her bath in the morning and was outside hanging up her washing. Mira was in the kitchen when she heard a thud. She thought it was from the upstairs flat as the people there are very uncivilized and always making some noise or the other. It was only after she came out of the kitchen that she saw Samdhinji lying outside. But by then, it was too late. Papa and I are on our way there now. You should go now too. I had planned to go shopping with Nishu, and now we will have to go in the afternoon when the shops are really crowded. How inconvenient!'

Everyone was upset to hear the unexpected news.

'She was the last person from that generation in the

family,' mourned Chachiji. 'All her brothers and sisters and their husbands and wives passed away at young ages. Now even she is gone.'

It appeared that the deceased was a distant relation of Chachiji's mother and therefore, she told Pranab, she thought it her duty to pay her respects to the departed soul without regard for the misfortune that might befall her if she went to a house of death at this crucial time in her daughter's life.

'No, no, Chachiji,' said Pranab on cue. 'Why should you bring bad luck to Pinky when she was such a distant relation? I too, am only going to drop Anu at the house. She can come back by rickshaw. Anu, hurry up and get ready.'

Anu rushed through a quick bath and wore a light pink sari as the white sari she kept for such occasions had not been ironed. Pranab was starting the car when they saw Gautam coming in through the gate, accompanied by a slim woman in a salwar kameez. Pranab stopped the car to tell him they were going to Mira Lall's house as her mother-in-law had passed away.

'It's all right, Bhaiyya, we just took a chance. This is my wife, Megha.'

Anu said, 'It is just next door. Would you like to come with us?'

Gautam flashed his delightful smile, 'Why not? I can meet several relatives there at the same time. Hop in, Megha.' He held the door open for her and almost tucked her in, moving her chunni away from the door before shutting it and loping round to the other side to get in.

'So what brings you to Patna, Gautam?' Pranab asked, putting the car in gear.

'Bhaiyya, actually Megha and I want to adopt a baby and we are looking for an adoption agency here,' he replied.

There was a short silence as Anu and Pranab absorbed this unusual bit of information. Gautam, by now used to the dropped jaws that greeted his announcement, was amused. He realized that people often didn't know how to respond, whether with delight or with sympathy. He looked across at Megha to share the moment with her, but she was staring out the window. 'Do you know of any adoption centres in Patna?'

It was Anu who replied. 'I don't think there are any agencies here. You should try hospitals; they sometimes have female babies left behind by their mothers.'

'We don't want an informal arrangement. We want to do it properly and legally so that there are no hassles later.'

'You should look for one in Delhi. I am sure they have agencies there,' Pranab suggested.

'We did. The waiting period is very long. We were hoping for something quicker here.'

'We could ask around, but the only person we know who adopted a baby is Mira di's brother-in-law in Hazaribagh. I don't think they went to any agency though. Perhaps now that they are coming here, you could ask them.' Pranab glanced in his rear-view mirror and saw Gautam and Megha exchange a look.

'I know Aditya bhaiyya is also involved in a lot of social activities and we could ask him,' Anu volunteered.

'Aditya?' Pranab was hesitant as he thought of his college mate. 'He only does research work for a social development institution to earn extra money,' he said, turning into the narrow lane to Mira di's house.

Amma had not arrived yet. They walked through the open door into the main hall. The furniture had already been moved into other rooms and the body was laid out in the centre, covered with a white sheet. There had not yet been time to enlarge and frame a photo of the departed lady, but there were some white rajnigandha stalks and marigolds strewn on the sheet and a few drooping stalks in a jug. A bunch of incense sticks sent up a spiral of smoke and scented the room. A small music system placed on the floor played mournful devotional songs.

Sheets had also been spread out all over the room and were occupied by grim adults, men squatting uncomfortably on one side and women huddled on the other. Close family members sat next to the body and occasionally, someone would start weeping loudly. Mira di sat red-eyed at the head as the eldest daughter-in-law.

Anu went and touched her on the shoulder and sat next to her for a moment.

'I didn't see her fall,' Mira di wept. 'I thought it was a sound from the first-floor flat.'

'Nobody can stop someone whose time has come,' said Pratibha didi, another cousin, sitting close by. 'It is all the will of god. Who are we mortals to stop him?'

Anu and Megha joined the ladies and found places on the sheet next to Pratibha didi. They sat quietly for a while, listening to the music. 'The other sons have not arrived yet,' Pratibha didi whispered. 'But one has already caught the flight from Calcutta and the other is driving from Hazaribagh, so they both should be here by the time of the cremation. The daughter is in England, so she obviously cannot make it in time.'

'Yes, it's not possible to wait in this season,' Anu whispered back. Then, seeing Pratibha didi eye the stranger in their midst, she introduced the young girl. 'This is Megha. She is the wife of Gautam Saran, Dr Biplab Kumar Prasad's grandson. They live in Delhi.'

Pratibha didi's face cleared. The introduction was enough to remind her of all the details of Gautam's family and marriage. 'So you are visiting here? It must be the first time after your marriage. And how is Bikram bhaisaab?'

Megha smiled uncertainly. 'He is fine, thank you.'

'He also doesn't come to Patna any more since Dr Prasad passed away even though Reemu still has so many relatives here.'

'Papa and Mummy don't like to travel much,' Megha said. 'And they go to America for two months every year to meet Bhaiyya and Bhabhi.'

Pratibha didi nodded. 'How is your health these days? I heard you had some problems.'

Megha seemed disconcerted by a total stranger seeming to know all about her. 'I had a sore throat before coming to Patna, but I am fine now, thank you.'

Fortunately, Amma arrived just then. After paying her respects, she seated herself next to Anu and immediately identified Megha. 'So you are Gautam's wife. How is Reemu? Is she here or in America?'

'In America,' replied Megha.

'So that is why you are visiting Patna. I met Gautam at Anu's house. He has become a fine young man. I was meeting him after a long time but I recognized him immediately. Where is he working?'

'With Genpact.'

'Ah,' Amma replied, as if she not only knew what it was but had no great opinion of it either. 'So have you paid your respects to all the family members?'

'We went to Nalanda and Rajgir,' mumbled Megha.

'Where is Babu?'

Megha started to disclaim all knowledge of any Babu but then realized that the question was for Pratibha didi.

'Babu has gone to make arrangements for the cremation,' Pratibha didi replied. 'The family pandit is out of town so he has to find another one for the last rites. The cremation will be held this afternoon. Mira's daughter, the one who lives with that girl in the south, has been informed,' she added with a meaningful look.

'Who is getting the food for the family? The fires must have been turned off after the death,' Amma said, deliberately ignoring the meaningful look, thereby implying that this was hardly the time or place for gossip about the poor girl's sexual preferences.

'I brought tea and biscuits for them but they are simply not interested in eating anything. I think the others from Babu's family are arranging lunch. After all, the children have to eat.'

The smaller children of various close relatives could be heard squealing in the next room, oblivious to the tragedy.

'I left in such a hurry that I could not prepare anything. I wanted to take Nishu shopping for the gifts for the engagement ceremony, but I had to come here instead. Patel Nagar is so far away...'

Fearing that Amma might feel obliged to offer dinner on her behalf, Anu rose to leave. 'I must return home,' she excused herself to Amma. 'Kallu chacha has gone to meet some people and will be home soon and Chachiji is alone.'

'Yes, yes, you have to cook lunch before the children return home,' agreed Amma.

Megha rose too and went to look for Gautam.

'I met quite a few relatives I never knew I had,' Gautam commented with a wry smile at Anu as they left the house. 'It's interesting that relationships are still valued. I like being recognized wherever I go, it is so different from Delhi.'

Manvi drove up in a red Swift while they were waiting for a rickshaw. She stopped the car in the middle of the road, got out and strode up to Anu. Without bothering to smile or greet her, she demanded, 'When is Girish arriving? What are his flight details?'

Anu shrugged. 'Sorry, Pranab has the information.' And even if I knew, I wouldn't tell you, her body-language conveyed.

'Well, if he is coming tomorrow, he must be on the one o'clock Delhi flight. Here is my cell number. Ask Pranab to give me a call about the flight. I want to go to the airport to receive Girish. He is such an old friend. We have so much to catch up on.' Ignoring Gautam and Megha, she spun off towards the house to pay her respects.

Gautam raised an eyebrow. 'Who was that?' he asked Anu.

'Someone who was in college with Pranab,' she replied shortly. Gautam let the matter drop.

When Anu returned home, Pinky was in the kitchen with the eggplant and potatoes already diced and the garlic and ginger ground with the other spices.

'I told her to prepare lunch,' said Chachiji, 'or she would have been too distracted after meeting that young boy. What did that boy Gautam want from you? Was that his baniya wife with him? She looks very nice.'

Anu, already annoyed with Manvi, muttered incoherently and escaped into the bathroom to change her sari. By the time she emerged, Pinky had the pressure cooker on the stove and was diligently frying the spices. It was a little difficult to do so without getting 'distracted' with Chachiji hovering around her, wondering aloud every few seconds what Kallu chacha was doing and when he would be back.

Fortunately, the maid distracted Chachiji. She was as interested in hearing every detail of the previous evening as Chachiji was in relating it. 'These days the boy's opinions are very important.' Chachiji told the maid.

'Mai-baap ke kauno baat na chalee,' the maid agreed. 'For my daughter, it was the boy who okayed the match after talking to her for a few minutes. And why would he not be impressed? She is such a sober, simple, hard-working girl. My younger daughter, though she is good-looking, wants to spend all her time with her creams and lipsticks and jewellery. She has taken after me in looks but not in sense.'

Anu remembered Pinky's computer course and asked her to turn on the computer so she could check her e-mail. She still felt hesitant about using the machine, afraid that she would accidentally delete everything on it. There were two messages from Girish sir.

Dear Anu,

Have you noted down the details of your societal interaction in the past week? That will help jumpstart my research in Patna. If you can persuade other women of your community to do the same, it would be immensely useful.

Hope to hear from you soon.
Girish

Dear Anu,

You didn't tell me what Transformer your son wants.

Girish

Anu, more familiar with the keyboard than before, quickly typed out her reply.

Dear Sir,

I am sorry I could not reply earlier. We've been very busy the past few days. The boy's side agreed to see Pinky so there was a lot of work to be done to clean up the house and arrange food for the meeting. It went off well and last night the boy's father called Kallu chacha to discuss the final details. He has gone there now and Chachiji is in great suspense.

Then I had to go to my cousin's house as she just lost her mother-in-law. She always used to complain about her, about how irritating she was, and how she constantly interfered in everything. Every time I met Mira di, she had a new story to relate about the problems she suffered because of her mother-in-law. And today, when the old woman died, Mira di was devastated. I think some of us like to be defined by our difficulties.

I met another young woman who you could talk to. Megha. She has come to Patna for the first time with her husband. They got married a few years ago against the wishes of their families. They are here to look for a baby they can adopt. This is quite unusual. The only other person we know who has adopted a child is Mira di's brother-in-law and that was done with great secrecy. Of course, everyone knows about it.

Megha would be able to give you a different point of view since most of the ladies I know are from my community. We seem to be limited to only a larger extended family for social interaction.

I hope you will find my suggestions useful.

And then, because Manvi had so irritated her with her overbearing self-confidence, she added,

I also met Manvi Prasad. She insists on going to the airport to receive your flight for old times' sake. Although you seem keen to excise her from your life, pretending that you barely remember her, she is still interested in your well-being. Perhaps she thinks you can start again from where you left off?

With kind regards,
Anu

Hitting 'send' made her feel better for a moment, until she realized that it would have no impact on Manvi's attitude, and she wondered what the poor man would think when he read the last paragraph.

Kallu chacha returned home close to lunchtime, putting an end to the cozy chat of the two disparate women, the maid squatting on the floor and Chachiji on the sofa, getting her feet massaged. Kallu chacha was in a state of high excitement and proudly exhibited a box of sweets which, though small, represented great delight.

'Have a sweet, everyone, today is a day for celebration! I took a box of sweets to Sahay saab in the morning and before he could say anything, I stuffed a sweet in his mouth! Then the cousin came out and ek-tho mithai okhra ke bhi de-deni, right in his mouth! Sahay saab had a long list of items in his pocket. He said his son had forbidden him to take dowry, but he had not said anything about things for the house. So he took out his list. Santro, fridge, TV and air-conditioner—all Samsung—sofas for the boy's clinic and the house, two sets of bedroom furniture, Godrej almirahs, three sets of gold jewellery, saris and Raymond suits for fifteen aunts and uncles and one lakh for their expenses.'

Chachiji, who had been standing, holding the box of sweets and munching on one, gulped and flopped onto the sofa. 'But we don't have so much saved,' she wailed. 'Pinky, beta, we will have to sell our house and withdraw money from the provident fund. We will have nothing left!'

'Oh!' remonstrated Kallu chacha, just as two large teardrops rolled down Pinky's cheeks. 'First listen to what I have to say, then start your wailing. So I told Sahay saab that I was only a retired government servant who had been honest to the bone all his life, and I could not afford a car and so much money. I said I had some money saved for Pinky's marriage and I could buy the sofa and one bedroom set and the fridge, but not the AC. I told him to spare us the three jewellery sets and reduce the money amount.

'He said he had received many offers from people for crores but ours was a reputable family, related to Avdhesh Saran's family, and that was the main consideration. But what could he do, he also had obligations. I talked to him agreeably for a while, impressing upon him that it was only forward-looking families like ours that could change outmoded ways of thinking. He agreed to leave the car out and came down to seventy-five thousand cash and two jewellery sets. But the suits and furniture he could not compromise on. Then, as we continued discussing, who should come in but Amitabh himself. He touched my feet and said pranam, such a polite, well-behaved boy he is. Then, seeing I was in such agitation, he asked what we had been talking about. His father tried to say it was nothing at all, kuchho naikhe, just discussions about the wedding time and other things. But hum-hoo kahani, it was not possible to discuss the time for the wedding yet until the gifts were finalized. The boy asked what gifts, and I said all this furniture and jewellery and clothes. He said he had to speak to his father and they went into the next room. I could hear them talking but I couldn't hear what they were saying and they took a long time. When they returned, Sahay saab was looking very unhappy and then I knew everything was going to be all right. Amitabh said he had some money saved up and they would be able to manage and there was no question of taking any gifts—money for the reception or clothes or furniture or anything at all. She will come only with the clothes she wants to wear, he said, and even that I can buy for her if she wants.

'See what a proper education can do? See what a boy learns when he goes to England? What a sensible boy, what a gem of a person! Oh, Pinky beta, you are so lucky!'

He dabbed at his eyes and Chachiji burst into unashamed tears and Pinky also started crying. Anu went into the kitchen to rescue the eggplant which by this time had probably become mush. It was almost time for the children to come home.

She heard Kallu chacha make plans to take the evening bus to Ranchi and start consultations with the family pandit. There was no time to be wasted, so as soon as Pranab returned from the bank, he would ask him to drive them to the bus stand.

Anu mentally crossed her fingers; plans could change at a moment's notice. And since Arnab had his maths test the next day, she could not even think of doing anything other than standing over him while he studied.

11

Badki Nani

GAUTAM WAS NOT the type to relax when there was work to be done. But he had enjoyed the visit to Mira Lall's place. He liked meeting people and observing their little quirks and mannerisms. He found Kallu chacha and Amma very entertaining with their constant tussles, while Pranab seemed stolid and reliable. With Anu, he experienced a conspiratorial friendship because she had a similar way of observing people, although he realized that she did so unconsciously, and would have been offended if he had pointed out that she laughed at her relatives.

After lunch in the dingy dining room of the public sector corporation guesthouse, he wanted to visit the hospital, with the hope that authorities there might have some information.

But Megha did not seem too keen.

'Maybe we aren't meant to be parents,' she said when they were back in the room.

Gautam wondered whether she was spiralling into one of her black moods, but she seemed her normal self. 'There is no such thing as "meant". I believe that one's life is a consequence of one's own choices.'

'Yes, but if one is striving and still not getting the desired results, one has to think of alternatives,' Megha pointed out. 'At some stage, one has to make a decision about how far to go and when to stop.'

'Well, we are just on vacation here and we haven't spent that much time striving yet.'

'But is it worth it? How do you know that an adopted child is what we really want?'

For a moment, Megha thought she saw a look of intense anger cross Gautam's face. But she was sure she was mistaken. Gautam never got angry, he was the most even-tempered person she knew.

'I thought you didn't doubt this decision?' he said finally.

'I don't,' she replied. 'Only, we have gone through a lot of effort, both in Delhi and here, but nothing seems to be happening.'

Gautam looked at her for a moment. Then he lay down on the bed, propped up a pillow against the headboard, and gestured to her to join him.

'I never told you the story of Badki Nani,' he began when she was snuggled close to him, her head on his shoulder. 'Do you remember I took Mummy to meet her when Mummy wanted to know more about the whole adoption thing? You couldn't come because you had to go shopping for your niece's birthday party. Badki Nani is not my real Nani, of course, but we always called her that because she was Nani's friend from school. I guess in those days girls hardly went to school, but Nani and Badki Nani had become fast friends before Badki Nani was married off at the age of thirteen. Nani was much younger so she remained in school for a while and when she herself got married a few years later, she found herself living right opposite Badki Nani. Their relationship was so strong throughout their life that we never realized they were not actually related.

'Badki Nani's son Lalit and his wife Amita had adopted a baby girl a long time ago and so I took Mummy to meet them. When I called Lalit mama, he told me his daughter was engaged. He was delighted to know that I was also considering the option and strongly encouraged me. He himself was going to be out of town for a few days—he is a consultant—but we could meet his mother any time.

'So I called Badki Nani.'

I'm *coming*, I'm coming, no need to keep ringing the doorbell. I'm not deaf! Where *is* that lazy servant, why isn't he opening the door...

Oh! It's Reemu! And your son. What is your name, beta? Gautam? Come in, come in. And here's the stupid Pappu. Why can't you tell me when you have to go get the milk, you silly boy. What if someone rings the bell, like Gautam bhaiyya here... how will *I* know you are not at home, eh? Now go and make some tea for Reemu bua and Gautam bhaiyya.

Come beta, sit here. Nihar and Amita have gone shopping. That girl, she is so excited about the marriage that she forgets everything else. I spoke to her on the mobile. She is stuck in traffic. Then she is going to meet Varun. They are going out together afterwards. Of course, in our days, we didn't even see each other till we got married, but nowadays, boys and girls from some families go out alone even if they are not thinking of getting married. Hai, we couldn't *imagine* such things when we were their age. Nihar is a very good girl; she would never go out with a boy if she was not planning to marry him and we have brought her up to respect family traditions. It is so important to maintain the *culture* of the family, otherwise we would be like everyone else, sending our daughters out with men they don't know, becoming too *modern*.

Pappu, you forgot to bring the *biscuits*! No, don't go now, serve Bua and Bhaiyya the tea first or it will get cold. Beta, how much sugar should I put? Only half a teaspoon! I cannot have my tea unless it has *three* spoons of sugar. What are you standing here for? Go and fetch the biscuits, those nice ones that Amita got from the bakery last week. Finished? What do you mean? Did you eat them all up already! Yes, blame it on Didiji, she never eats biscuits, she is so thin, the poor girl. I keep telling her she needs her strength for the marriage, but when does she ever listen to me. Okay, don't just *stand* here. Fetch the biscuits from the packet.

Nobody listens to me at all, not even this miserable young boy. Illiterate and dull, yet he wants to use his own brains. What brains did god give you, I ask him. Amita says I shouldn't scold him, but if I don't scold then how will he learn his work? It is for his own good that I scold him. Young people should listen to their elders who have much more experience.

But at times... yes, occasionally, even elders may be mistaken. Amita didn't listen to me, you know, when...

You want to know about Nihar, don't you? I told Amita she shouldn't tell Nihar anything about her adoption, but she insisted she couldn't keep such a big secret from her own daughter. Amita always does what she wants. When she wanted to get a baby from the centre, I said she shouldn't, but she didn't listen and later I realized it was a good thing she didn't.

Varun is an intelligent young man, I know that. I am so glad Nihar met him, she needed an intelligent solid young man with a good job, like him. Look at me! Crying! But it's so wonderful that she will be going to her own house now, where she belongs. Our responsibility will be over at last and we can hand her to the boy forever.

How was I to know... I told Amita that she was still young and she would have her own baby when it was god's wish. To even *think* of getting a child from a centre!

But what can you say to these girls of today. I told Amita about Gunjan mama's wife, who had twins after twelve years of marriage, though they were girls. There are so many women who give birth, by god's grace, later in life, why should *she* go rushing ahead after only eleven years of marriage. But she! She said eleven years were long enough and she was not going to wait for something that may never even happen and reach the end of her life without having a child.

What kind of baby will you get from the centre, I asked her, how do you know if it will be healthy? She said that the doctors at the centre would make sure of that. Besides, she said, where is the guarantee that any child I give birth to will be healthy? Yes, I said, but at least it will be your own god-given child and whatever problem it has will be given by god to you. God makes all children, Amma, she said. But why should you deliberately go and get a child with a health problem? It just doesn't make sense, have you thought about who will look after it? I am getting old now, I can't look after an unhealthy little baby from nowhere, all the babies at these kinds of places are unhealthy; you just don't know what disease they may be carrying.

Amma, no baby comes free of illnesses. My grandfather had diabetes, my grandmother's brother died very young due to a heart disease, your mother's sister had a skin disease... any child of our family would be prone to these diseases.

But how will you know if the baby is from a *good* family?

What is a good family, Amma?

A family like *ours*, of course... cultured, well-educated, from a high caste, of high morals and values. Like you, beta.

Amma, my grandmother was illiterate. In those days, they didn't send girls to school. Actually, if you go back a little further, my ancestors were all unlettered, uncultured. They had no land and too many mouths to feed in the village. My grandfather was the first to come to a city to get an education and a job. We will never know the caste of the baby from the centre, not even the religion maybe, but she will become our family and therefore, our caste.

What, not even a *Hindu*! I cannot allow that. You

can't do this, I will speak to Lalit, he can't allow this! Oh, what will people say! No one will speak to me again.

For many days afterwards I couldn't even sleep. But Lalit told me I should let Amita do what she wanted. What could I do? I even mentioned it at my Thursday kirtana group, to my friends who sing there. I had to, so that everyone would be prepared for this strange thing that she was doing. In fact, it was they who reassured me. They reminded me of Sita Mata herself, who was picked up from a field by Raja Janak. Who knew where she came from, they asked me. Well, I replied, from the earth, of course, she was a daughter of the earth. That is only to explain to illiterate people, said Ambikaji, we *educated* people realize that she must have been adopted. And what about Krishna Bhagwan. Wasn't he brought up by Yashodha Maiyya, while his own mother was in jail? These days, they told me, things like caste and family are not so important anyway. Do we know who is travelling in the same train compartment as us, whether they are Brahmins or Harijans? Do our sons ask about caste when they go to look for a job? Even when they bring home *foreigners* as wives, we can't say anything. We have to adjust with the times, they said, otherwise our children will reject us.

It was okay for them to talk, *their* daughters-in-law were not going to get babies from the centre. But I listened and didn't say anything. But I didn't go with Amita and Lalit when their turn came after a long wait and they had to go and look at the babies. Do what you like, I told them, it's your life. But don't expect *me* to look after this baby, I am too old now.

They chose a girl. A girl! A girl is such a *burden*. Such a problem to marry off, with dowry so *high* these days. And they can't look after you in your old age. A son's house is your house, but daughters go away after marriage to their own homes and you can't stay with them! Why, I didn't even like to drink water in any of my daughters' houses. Nowadays though, I sometimes go and stay with them when they insist strongly. They tell me I am too old-fashioned, and my grandchildren also like me to stay with them. But I am never comfortable and I stay only for a few days. It is not possible also, because it is so *expensive* buying chocolates or sweets or fruits every day for my sons-in-law and grandchildren.

You should have seen Amita, she was so excited the day they went to get the baby home. What a glow on her face, what sparkle in her eyes! And all for an unknown child from a centre. For days, she had been shopping for the baby. Tiny dresses, delicate woollens, embroidered sheets, lacy blankets, bottles, nappies, powder, baby oil, cotton wool, so many many things, even a pram and a cot. In our days, babies slept on sheets made of old saris and wore clothes other babies had grown out of. Lalit even hired another maid to do the washing and mind the baby. He moved his study table into another room to make place for the cot. I had to help them arrange the baby's things on the table near the cot because Amita was doing it all wrong. Nappies should *always* be on top because they are used the most for newborns.

Amita's parents and her brother and his wife and my younger daughter and her husband, all went to the centre to get the baby. The children waited here, all very excited. They took her to the mandir nearby before they brought her home. They entered the house and touched my feet. Amita was crying. The baby was in my daughter's arms. Then I saw Nihar for the first time.

What a tiny little body! Such big eyes, so dark and intense. She was two months old, Lalit told me. Her eyes fixed on me and her lips moved. Look, Amma, my daughter pointed, look, she smiled at you! This is her first smile since we saw her. Then everyone gathered around the little bundle and tried to make her smile again.

I knew it wasn't a smile, babies of that age don't know how to smile, but nobody believed me. Everyone was so thrilled, I couldn't even say anything when they pushed the baby at me. I had to take her in my arms. Then the children shouted, Show her the house, Naniji, show her her new home, and they made me follow them around the whole house, and pointed out her cot and her toys, and they had even got her some gifts. I told them she won't even *understand*, but children are children.

That night, she wouldn't go to sleep. Amita walked around with her for a long time, patting her and giving her the bottle, even singing to her. But nothing worked, the baby was still awake. I said it must be because it's a new place and the child is not used to it. She put the baby in the cot, but then she started crying, so again she had to pick her up and walk her up and down, up and down, and nobody was getting any sleep. Finally, I had to take her from Amita and then she was asleep in *two minutes* in my arms. You were holding her all wrong, I told her. Now we can put her in the cot, she said. Don't be silly, I told her, she will wake up again the moment she is in the cot. I kept her with me, hugging her close to me until I was sure she was fast asleep, only then did

I put her in the cot. She was clutching my sari so tightly, Amita had to carefully unwrap her little fingers from it before we could let go of her.

Call her again, beta, it shouldn't take her so long...

Stopped at another shop? Did you tell her you were waiting here? Something important? Oh, all right...

You know, beta, there is so much love within a baby. We think they are too small, they have no emotions, they smile when their tummies are full and cry when they are hungry or wet. We think they don't notice who is around them, who is looking after them, they don't know who their mothers are, who their families are, they don't know who loves them and whom they should love.

But now I realize that a baby knows *everything*! That Nihar, she would cry every time the maid came near her and she wouldn't be quiet until Amita was with her. I was amazed. How did this baby know who her mother was? And it was true, she smiled at me, she was happy to see me, and when she grew older, she would hold out her arms to come to me. How did she know I was her grandmother?

God is in every child, beta, and a baby is the purest form of god. A baby can give so much love to those around it. Just by being quiet in your presence, just by eating and drinking what you give it, just by looking at you with its sleepy eyes, just by trusting you enough to fall asleep in your arms.

I'll tell you honestly, I had my doubts. But there was such a difference in the house after Nihar came. I saw Lalit smile again, his real smile, not the tired polite smile he had developed over the years. I realized how much he had changed over the years, as if a veil had gradually settled on him, making him weary and irritable. And now it was as though the veil had disappeared overnight and he was once again what he was meant to be, the enthusiastic, curious, loving person he really was.

And what else did that tiny little baby do by just being there? She turned us into a family again. Before she came, we were three old people living together, with nothing to talk about any more, and nothing to keep us close. We had separated into individuals. Children make a family, they give it unity and purpose. Now we sat together and marvelled at Nihar, admired her every gesture, worried together when she didn't eat or when she was unwell, laughed and pointed out her antics to each other.

That is the real marvel of children... they grab you by the heart and make you theirs without thinking about whether or not you want them at all. Their undemanding love for you, their very need for you, their dependence attracts even the most reluctant person to them. There is no option but to love them back.

People might think that an adopted child is different. But let me tell you what happened when Nihar was seven years old. Amita used to take Nihar for the fancy-dress competition at the club every Christmas. The first year, she was a dancer, just over a year old and she had barely learned how to walk. Amita got her a lehenga-choli and put make-up on her and she looked so *pretty*.

When she got older, she decided on her own what she wanted to be and she and her mother would design the costume. When she was five, she was a *witch*! I told her, you look so scary that I am scared you will eat me right up! She laughed and laughed and pretended to pounce on me to eat me up. I had to pretend to run away, and when she caught me, she hugged me tightly and said, But I will never eat *you*, Dadi.

When she was seven, she decided to be a fairy. How excited she was!

Reemu, do you want something? Some more tea? A cold drink? Okay... oh, Pappu, come here quickly! Pappu! Where is that boy? What took you so long? Go and get a Coca Cola for Bua and Bhaiyya, and get it in that nice glass Amita uses for guests. Don't forget to put ice in it. What, you don't want ice, beta? Okay... Pappu! Don't put ice in the glass!

Let me tell you the story of the fancy-dress competition.

Nihar told her mother, we can cut the wings from some nice lacy cloth, Mamma, and then we can buy a lovely new dress for me, a pink one, no, a white one, and white ballet shoes, and we can make a wand with Dadi's knitting needle. Won't it look lovely, Mamma, won't I look nice?

You will look beautiful, her mother told her. But we can't buy a new white dress for you just now. How about the pretty blue dress Bua gave you for your birthday?

But Nihar insisted on a new dress. I want a white dress, fairies don't wear blue clothes!

Tell you what, said her mother, we can tie your hair with a white lacy scarf, and we can put stars on it, little silver stars. And a big silver star on Dadi's knitting needle. Then you will be a beautiful blue and white fairy.

And I can put stars on my *new ballet shoes* as well! Nihar said.

Oh Pappu, I told you not to put ice in Bhaiyya's Coca Cola! Can't you ever listen to what I say! Go. Take the ice cubes out. And use a clean spoon!

She was being so clever, if she couldn't have a new dress, at least she wanted a definite promise about the new shoes! When Amita kept quiet, I said, new shoes will be much too expensive, your black school shoes will do fine, but Amita mentioned that the old ballet shoes were fraying so she had to buy new ones in any case. Nowadays, parents spoil their children so much, indulging in their every desire.

They spent days decorating a pretty blue dress with silver paper stars, and made wings of cellophane, decorated with more silver stars. They bought new shoes and a white scarf. Nihar tried on the clothes and preened in front of the mirror, trying out different kinds of walks, swinging her hips, practising her songs. It was such fun watching her. She would walk up to the mirror, sing a song, wave her wand, then say, 'Dadi, now you must clap!' I used to watch her from the bed, because I was ill those few days, but I clapped hard every time, because she put in so much effort and because she did it so well. You will get the first prize, I told her.

On the day of the fancy-dress competition, Lalit had to go out of town. In the morning, when Nihar was in school, Amita took me to the doctor who said I would have to take antibiotics because it was a viral infection. He also gave me the other medicine which makes me so sleepy I feel like closing my eyes even when I am standing.

I had my medicines after lunch and then naturally, I lay down on my bed and went to sleep. I knew that

Amita and Nihar would get ready for the competition and go to the club in the afternoon. I told Nihar to have a good time and to show me the prize when she came home. Then I dozed off.

When I awoke, it was already dark. You know how early it becomes dark during winter. The curtains were pulled and there was no light coming through the windows. Meena, I called, Meena! Where are you! *Hurry up.*

Nihar hurried into the room. What do you want, Dadi, she asked. Do you want a glass of water? Should I ask Mummy to make your tea?

No, no, I said. It will be dinnertime soon. Did you eat something at the club? Show me your prize. What did you get this year?

We didn't go, Dadi, she said.

I was *shocked*. My heart jumped.

Why, what happened, are you all right? Is Mummy all right? And Lalit!... Lalit is fine, isn't he?

She was puzzled. Of course we are all all right, Dadi. Nothing happened. Was something going to happen? What was going to happen, Dadi?

Nothing was going to happen, I reassured her hastily, mystified. But didn't you go for the fancy-dress competition at the club, I asked her.

No, she said, as if she had never planned to go. I will get you a glass of water, then I will tell Mummy to make your tea. Meena has gone to buy vegetables.

Then she went away. I lay back and thought it must have been a dream. The fancy-dress competition is on at the club. Nihar is on stage, wearing the fairy dress she decorated so painstakingly, singing her song and waving her wand and swinging her little hips. I hope everyone claps as loudly as I am clapping because otherwise she will be so disappointed. And if she doesn't get a prize, she will cry and cry. Then I will take her in my lap and tell her it doesn't matter, that I thought she was the best, that she tried her best, and I will tell her I will beat the judges with a big stick and tell them that my little Nihar was the best little girl on stage. Then she will laugh and laugh and feel better and go out to play. I must have been missing my little fairy so I must have just imagined she was right here with me. Now I must wake up and tell that Meena to switch on the light and get me my tea.

But it was Amita who came into the room carrying a cup of tea.

Where is Meena? Why are *you* bringing my tea? You were supposed to go for the fancy-dress to the club!

Nihar didn't want to go, she told me.

But she was so excited about it! What happened? Did she suddenly become shy?

No, replied Amita, Nihar said she couldn't leave you here, alone and sick.

Alone and sick? But I am not alone. Meena was here with me.

She said you might wake up and have high fever, Amita told me. Meena wouldn't be able to give you your medicine.

But you should have insisted! She should have gone! I would have been all right. Why did she *miss* the competition? Why didn't you *insist*?

I didn't insist because I knew she was right, Amita said. I should have thought of it myself, but I didn't want to disappoint her. I asked several times if she was sure

SHARMILA KANTHA

she didn't mind missing the competition. She was sure, she couldn't leave you here alone when you were sick.

Then Nihar called her from the other room and she put the tea on the table and left. She forgot to switch on the light. I sat there in the darkness, and the tea became cold, but I couldn't drink it. I was choked with tears. I am just an old woman, beta, and nobody wants old people any more. We are a burden on society, we are alone and helpless, as dependent as little children. And who has the time to sit with us now? I can't blame anybody because I can see how busy life has become. My son is always working and Amita is always doing some household chore, they both work so hard. Who has the time to spend a few minutes talking to an old person? And what do I know anyway? The times have moved on, things are no longer the same, so who am I to tell them what they should be doing? I just sit here and pass time until god decides to send for me.

When a child shows so much love and sacrifice, it touches the heart forever, it leaves a mark. I sit here and sometimes when I am alone, I think of that day when my little Nihar gave up her fancy-dress prize just to be with me, and my mind glows and I tell god, if you take me today, I will die a happy old woman.

That must be her! Pappu, Pappu! Open the door quickly! Didiji has come and Bhaiyya is waiting. Where are you? Hurry up!

❦

Gautam held Megha closer. 'Amita mami was right. She said there were no guarantees. We have to work our way around every imperfection we come across in our lives. Is any relationship perfect? Is any job perfect? Any place? Any home? We make our compromises. We do the best we can under given circumstances. We can't search for a dream that might elude us all our life, that will drain us drop by drop with every disappointment. We must take control of our happiness.'

Megha sighed and shifted on Gautam's shoulder. 'I am happy. I am doing my best with all my imperfections.'

And Gautam felt the cold wetness of her cheek on his arm.

12

Rumours and Surmises

In a flurry of hectic activity, loud remonstrations and hurried farewells, Kallu chacha and family left the way they had arrived, complete with neatly packed plastic baskets and camouflage-covered suitcase.

Anu reserved her sigh of relief in case there were no tickets for the bus to Ranchi. Besides, she would be seeing plenty of Kallu chacha over the next few months as he frequented Patna for various marriage requirements.

Meanwhile, Arnab was still struggling with fractions. Keeping in mind her own frustrating problems in learning something new, Anu was less irritable in explaining. At the end of half an hour, Arnab and she had amicably gone through more sums than anticipated.

She checked her e-mail for the second time during the day.

Dear Anu,

I was surprised to read your mail. You seem to be under the impression that Manvi Prasad and I were close. As I recall, she was this rather tiresome, aggressive, overgrown teenager in need of constant attention. I have no inclination to meet her, especially if she is labouring under a twenty-year-old misapprehension.

Now I connect what you said earlier about everyone knowing why I left Patna. It certainly had nothing to do with Manvi Prasad, but do not expect me to go around explaining matters to people!

I am leaving the house now to catch my flight.

Look forward to meeting you.
Girish

Anu read the message several times in utter disbelief. The compelling rumour about the professor's infatuation with his student had been so well-entrenched in city folklore that the e-mail did not make any sense. She herself had obsessed over the romance for the past few days.

And now he was saying it wasn't even true. He was certainly not in a state of misery, denying the memories of a long-lost love. Clearly, his recollection of Manvi was hazy and imperfect. Anu had thought his e-mails reinforced the old story, but it seemed he really was entirely oblivious to Manvi's existence, and neither her name nor her fervent desire to meet him held any meaning for him at all, other than a mild irritation.

He had applied for a PhD, received a scholarship, borrowed money from his brother and left. Nothing more. And there was nothing in the city to tempt him to return, apart from several squabbling siblings and their cranky wives. But the familiarity of his hometown had been an advantage when he had to do this research, and so, quite simply, he was visiting for official work, work that was properly funded.

This unexpected revelation shook Anu to the core. Her belief in everlasting love and a simultaneous vague dissatisfaction with her own life, that had gathered strength since the announcement of the professor's arrival, now seemed to be an illusion. By association then, if the undying romance between the professor and his beautiful student was not real, could her own dissatisfaction be real?

He would be in Patna by lunchtime the next day. She would find time to explain to Pranab about his research work and her participation in it before he arrived. She sat in front of the computer, staring at the blank monitor, and focussed on rationalizing her emotions. Her husband was not demonstrative, but she knew that she was the most important person in his life. His family was his core, his friends could depend on him.

The doorbell rang. Anu opened the door, expecting Pranab to be back from the bus stop, but it was Gautam and Megha.

'Bhabhi, we are just coming from the hospital,' Gautam announced as soon as they entered. 'We went there as you had suggested. They referred us to a children's home where they send babies that are abandoned. Apparently, they get two or three cases like that every month.'

'Mostly, they are girls, but that's the case everywhere,' added Megha, her eyes shining. 'We spoke to the person in charge at the home. They said they have a baby girl who was left on the steps of a police station. She was just a few days old then, and has been with them for three weeks. They said she is in reasonably good health. It's not a registered agency, but they work with some other organization here in Patna.'

'We asked if we could come and see the baby and they agreed. So we are planning to go tomorrow,' Gautam continued, sounding excited.

The doorbell rang again and this time it was Pranab, fortunately without Kallu chacha in tow. It transpired that a bus to Ranchi had just been leaving and the driver was only too happy to fill up the vacant seats. So the camouflage-covered suitcase was flung onto the roof and the plastic baskets stowed under the seats and in the overhead shelf, Kallu chacha bought some samosas for the journey, Chachiji suddenly remembered she had left her comb in the children's room and yelled at Pranab from the window to make sure Anu kept it properly so they could take it on their next visit, Pinky touched his feet, and then the bus lumbered off into the night.

Dinner was already on the table and Anu asked Gautam and Megha to join them.

Pranab and Gautam talked about Gautam's job with a multinational firm, while the others listened and Anu served everyone. The children usually squabbled at dinnertime, but today they seemed quite fascinated by an actual account of outsourcing, India's most happening industry. Gautam told them about India's reputation abroad and how the country's knowledge economy was admired and respected all over the world, and how many of the top international companies were sending

their back-office work to India. Not only that, Gautam
went on, Indian companies were now buying foreign
companies and some had even become the largest in
the world. The future of India was changing rapidly and
by the time Radhika and Arnab were in the job market,
they would be able to name their price. Within a few
years, they would be earning in lakhs.

The children listened in open-mouthed disbelief.

Then it was time for the serials. Last evening's serials
had been abandoned halfway when Sahay saab had
called, but that was no major loss.

Matters were complicated in the serial about the
unmarried pregnant girl. The rapist, the distant admirer
and the lone policeman happened to meet in the club
bar and the conversation turned acrimonious. Most of
the episode was taken up by the policeman's innuendos
and oblique references which made the admirer feel he
was being accused of the crime, and he became more
and more agitated as the episode progressed. However,
before he could erupt violently, the credits rolled.

Before Megha and he left, Gautam requested Pranab
to accompany them to the children's home the next day.
'We would also like you to come with us, Bhabhi. You
will be able to give us some expert baby advice.'

Pranab seemed quite inclined to go as this was an
unusual venture.

'You have to go to receive the professor tomorrow,'
Anu pointed out.

'Yes, but this is in the same direction as the airport,
only a little further away. We can go to the airport on
our way back.'

'But I have to make lunch and get the house ready,'

said Anu, although she would really have liked to see the baby and the home.

'The house is fine. You can make lunch before we go,' Pranab insisted.

Gautam had already booked a car, an Ambassador, which would be large enough to take the four of them and have space for the professor as well as his luggage. Pranab decided to take the day off, so there would be no rush in the morning. Once Gautam and Megha left, Anu went to put the children to bed. Arnab had his maths test the next day and needed his sleep. Radhika had Hindi, but she, at least, was well prepared, despite the distractions of the previous week.

Anu cleaned up the kitchen, piled up the used dishes under the sink ready for the maid the next day, located all the necessary pieces of the children's uniforms and got the school bags ready. Then she went into her bedroom and after switching off all the lights, she turned towards her husband with a passion that was founded in a new certainty.

Later she told him about her e-mail contact with the professor and his request for help.

'That's a very good idea, Anu,' Pranab agreed. 'You know, I have recently felt that you have been wasting your time. The children are also growing up. You can't spend the rest of your life cooking and doing their homework.'

'But I have never worked. What can I do?' she protested.

'You have a master's degree in psychology. You could always get into social activity.'

'You mean, like Aditya?'

'Yes, why not? Do research work, I'll put you in touch with him, and if Girish sir likes your work, he can also put in a word here and there. I'm sure that with his reputation, a recommendation from him could really help. There are so many NGOs working seriously in Patna now. It's just a matter of getting into the system. Maybe they'll even offer you a salary!'

'Girish sir said that he didn't remember Manvi Prasad, unless she was that irritating student who always sought attention. Can you believe she was spreading false rumours about him all these years?'

'I am not at all surprised. I never believed in this scandal myself. Girish sir was not the type. And Manvi is truly irritating; she thinks she is this glamorous working woman and that all men fall for her. Totally self-deluded!'

'So you didn't get taken in by her like other men did? You didn't think she was attractive and desirable?'

Pranab snorted in disgust. 'Why should I when I have my own lovely wife to look at! Go to sleep and stop wondering about grand unrequited passions.'

With that, Pranab kissed her gently and snuggled into his pillow. Grand unrequited passions. Manvi Prasad had made up the entire story of the affair with Girish.

Perhaps it helped her define herself. Perhaps it built her confidence and made her feel unique.

Dismissing Manvi Prasad from her imagination at last, Anu happily remained awake for a while, considering her various options, dreaming about going to villages and working with women on health, education and empowerment. It seemed doable. It seemed exciting.

13

Wednesday

HE WAS ARRIVING today.

There was no time for further reflection. At the last moment, Arnab couldn't find his box of mathematical instruments, but was adamant that he needed it even though the test was on fractions. He refused to start getting dressed without his box and Anu had to beg Radhika to lend him hers, which she protested about as she claimed she needed it herself. Finally, Anu compromised by giving the box to Arnab with only a ruler and a pencil, and the protractor, compass and triangles to Radhika.

Amma called early in the morning, soon after the children left. Anu had had her bath and started cooking. Pranab was just rolling out of bed.

'I am going to Nishu's place soon. Munna has bought all the supplies for the cook and sent someone to buy the vegetables early in the morning so that they are fresh. We finally managed to complete the shopping for the gifts for the boy's family yesterday. These days, shopkeepers are so clever... they wrap everything beautifully. I told Nishu that they must be charging extra for it but we didn't have time to do it ourselves although Nanni could easily have done the packing instead of going with Gunni to the beauty parlour. Anyway, I told the shopkeeper to wrap the gifts in clear plastic so that everyone could see what was inside. What time will you come in the evening?'

Anu told her about the proposed expedition to the children's home and then the trip to the airport to pick up the professor from America.

'You should bring Giru to the function. Also bring Gautam and his wife. Nishu has asked the cook to prepare for a hundred and thirty people so there will be plenty of food. But come on time. As the girl's cousin, you will also have to look after the guests. Nanni and Manni are too young for it and there is nobody else from the family.'

Amma was in a hurry to leave so the conversation, fortunately, was short. She did not vent her views on the pros and cons of adoption or Anu being involved or the professor from America being a possible rapist.

Gautam and Megha arrived and they all piled into the Ambassador, Pranab in the front seat and Megha between Anu and Gautam in the back seat. The driver shot off at a terrific starting pace that had nearby rickshaws scurrying for cover.

'Driver, slow down!' Pranab exclaimed as he clutched at the dashboard. 'There is no hurry.'

The driver barely glanced his way and continued weaving erratically through the dense traffic.

'Bhaiyya, you heard Bhaisahab,' said Gautam sharply from the back seat. 'Go slow, please.'

The driver, with great reluctance, lifted his foot off the accelerator. In retaliation, he slowed to an unnecessarily sedate pace.

'These people think they own the roads and that others should just disappear from their path,' Pranab shook his head reprovingly.

Gautam replied, 'Traffic is worse in Delhi. Nobody seems bothered about rules. Even with a driver, I find myself constantly watching the road for careless traffic.'

'But at least you have wide roads and traffic lights. Here, most of the roads are congested and the lights don't even work.'

'When we were in the States, one couldn't drive over the speed limit even if there was no traffic for miles,' Megha added. 'Once, we drove through the Nevada desert and it seemed as if we were the only car on that long highway. And when we crossed the speed limit, suddenly there was this police car behind us. We were stopped and fined on the spot.'

'People would obey traffic regulations here also if there was anyone to enforce them,' Pranab asserted. 'But our law and order situation is so bad that people can get away with anything.'

The long journey passed with amicable discussions on various topics until finally the car swept through a gateway with no gate and braked to a stop in an area cleared of wild grass.

The building did not look at all promising. In the sudden stillness, they viewed it from the car for a moment before venturing out. It sat by itself in the centre

of a ground separated from the surrounding wilderness.
There were neat fields behind it, but in front, the grass
grew tall and untended. There was no boundary wall
or fence. The building was small, maybe two or three
rooms and a porch, painted a cheap dismal yellow. Large
parts of it were dilapidated and needed urgent rounds of
cementing. The windows were grimy and shut. One door
was open and through it a small dark room was visible.
A crooked board over the porch said in faded red letters
'Ashalaya Home'. A Gypsy car stood by the side of the
building looking as if it had survived many a pothole and
near mishap.

In the silence, a cacophony of children's voices could
be heard chanting by rote some lesson whose content
was indistinguishable. Then a man emerged from the
dingy interior.

'Kahiye, what do you want?' he asked, suspiciously,
as if they rarely had visitors.

'We want to meet Mrs Jha. Is she here?'

The man looked him up and down. 'Where have you
come from?'

'I spoke to her yesterday about the baby.'

The man perked up. 'Oh, about the baby. Come in,
she is here.' He came down the porch steps. 'My name is
Jaikishan Mishra. I am in charge here.'

He took them into the front room. There was a
wooden desk and a few plastic chairs, a bookshelf with
old dusty books and some paintings by children on the
walls which looked like they had been hanging there
for the past decade. A grimy curtain at the doorway
prevented them from seeing the rest of the house.

Mishra seated himself behind the desk and the visitors

took the plastic chairs. There were only three chairs, so Gautam sat on a trunk near the bookshelf.

'This is actually a school for poor children. Mrs Jha's father-in-law started it twenty years ago. Jhaji passed away several years ago and since then Mrs Jha has been looking after the affairs. She wanted to build a hostel for orphan children but there was no money for that. We are such an old institution, yet the government does not support our good work. We spend our own money and take in children who have no place to go. My wife looks after them. Right now, we have three children and this baby sent by the hospital.'

'How many children are studying here?' asked Gautam.

'It is always changing. Sometimes we have almost sixty or seventy. But in this season or when the rains come, there are only twenty or thirty. They don't come regularly. Children come for a year or two, then they start working and have no time to learn. This is a free school and we also provide books and slates, so they come when they feel like it. But no one is interested in learning for long.'

It was such a dismal picture that the visitors had nothing to say.

The chanting came to an end and a woman entered the room from the other side of the curtain.

'Gautamji? Namaste. I am Mrs Jha.' She was not young, but looked far from middle-aged. 'How did you like our school? It is only a small effort, but I am trying to get funds from the government so that we can expand and get more children in. Come, let me show you around.'

She moved energetically through the curtain. The others followed. They entered a corridor with two rooms leading off it. The rooms had no doors but were large and received light from windows on the opposite wall which were obviously kept clean for this purpose. A group of children, mostly boys of different ages, were seated on the floor in one room, dressed in faded blue uniforms that must have belonged to other students in other schools. The trousers, reaching only till the ankles of the wearers, were held up with pieces of string, the faded and torn shirts with missing buttons were clumsily tucked in. The children were unkempt and slouched disinterestedly over the slates in their laps. The arrival of the visitors aroused some movement and they looked up. Anu thought their eyes had no spark, no curiosity, no mischief that could be expected of children their age.

'Stand up. Say namaste,' ordered Mrs Jha. The children stood dutifully, folded their hands and mumbled something.

Gautam moved forward and patted some of them on the head. 'What are you studying? Do you like it?'

Some of the children, the younger boys, smiled at him, but there was no response to his question. Gautam crouched down beside an older boy and addressed him. 'What is your name?'

'Sanjay Kumar,' replied the boy formally, as if he wasn't used to giving his name.

'Where do you live, Sanjay?'

'Beluatar.'

'Do you come to school every day?'

'Yes,' was the confident reply and some of the children giggled at this obvious misrepresentation.

'No laughing,' Mrs Jha said sternly, and the laughter subsided.

'Doesn't matter,' said Gautam to Sanjay. 'But if you study hard you will get a good job.'

The children gaped at him with the same wide-eyed disbelief that Radhika and Arnab had shown the previous evening. There were too many youths who had passed class seven or eight, but still lounged about their villages without any employment prospects.

'Sit down. Be quiet,' bellowed Mrs Jha, and led the way out of the room.

Gautam couldn't resist a parting line of advice. 'The future is changing. Study hard so that you are ready for it.'

The children stared back uncomprehendingly, their little experience of life at odds with this statement.

The other room had a single string cot and some clothes thrown over a wire strung across the wall. The baby lay alone in the cot.

Gautam, Megha, Anu and Pranab gathered around the cot and looked down at the wriggling infant. She was wearing only a shift, but seemed quite active, flinging about her tiny arms and legs and making tiny sounds.

'My wife has just given her milk,' said Mishra from behind them.

They stood in silence, Anu unsure of what was expected of Pranab and her, and Pranab quite obviously out of his depth. Then Megha moved forward abruptly and picked up the baby. She held her close, supporting her head with the crook of her arm.

'Let's go,' she said clearly and walked out, through the dark corridor, into the dingy front room and down the porch to the car parked in the sunshine.

'But... but our money!' Mishra spluttered, following agitatedly.

'The formalities, our expenses, and what about the donation?' Mrs Jha exclaimed.

'I'll sort all that out right now,' Gautam said, reaching into his pocket for his wallet and stopping the two officials in their tracks. He wrote out a cheque and took out a wad of cash. The duo from the home accepted the ten thousand-rupee notes with alacrity and carefully scrutinized the cheque for fifty thousand.

The paperwork was going to be a little more difficult. Gautam's insistence on proper papers was most inconvenient. The home itself was in no position to provide any certifications since this was an entirely off-the-record favour they were doing for the hospital. They would have to go to the hospital and ask them to prepare backdated records of the baby's recovery, then get the police, the court, the adoption agency and other concerned departments to start the legal process. All this would require substantial effort but it could be accomplished if there was adequate compensation. In the meantime, the care of the baby could be handed over to Gautam immediately.

Mrs Jha, quite delighted with the morning's events, mentioned that she herself was on her way back to the city and would accompany the prospective parents to the hospital. So it was decided that Gautam, Megha and the baby would leave for the city in the Gypsy, which apparently worked despite its decrepit appearance, while the Ambassador would take Pranab and Anu to the airport to receive the professor.

The driver reversed the car out of the compound,

Pranab and Anu said goodbye to Gautam and Megha and left for the airport.

At the precise moment when the car started its journey, Bantu was untying Srijana's goat from its post near the road. Chintu and he had decided to give it a run around the village. They often did this as it was a challenge holding on to the frisky black goat as it raced about and they enjoyed the tussle. Besides, it was a good way to elicit envy from their friends.

Unfortunately, this time the goat got the better of them almost immediately and managed to free itself, running wildly around the village with the shouting children charging behind it.

And when the Ambassador reached the village crossing, the goat darted onto the road. The driver wrenched the wheel to the left and screeched to a stop at the side of the road, narrowly avoiding the goat, a man on a bicycle and the village well.

A red Swift coming from the other side was not so fortunate. In its effort to avoid the frantic goat, it rammed straight into a tree. The silence following the crash was awful.

Pranab raced out of his car to the red Swift. Anu recognized it as Manvi Prasad's car and realized she had been heading for the airport.

Behind the Ambassador, Mishra's Gypsy also braked sharply. Gautam was out and running to the afflicted car to help even before the Gypsy came to a halt.

Anu opened the door of the car and stepped out slowly.

It was like a TV serial. She could almost hear the loud dramatic music. There would be a close-up of her face.

Wide eyes, lips parted, slow motion. The imaginary camera swivelled around her surroundings, to record the evolving tableau.

At her side of the crossroads, Megha had opened the car door, she was sitting with the baby cradled against her chest, trying to protect it from the horrible sight of the crash. A woman can transform into a mother from one moment to the next. *Emphatic drumbeats. A close-up of Megha, then the baby, Megha, the baby...*

At the platform around the village well crouched a young woman. Her sari was clean, her hair neatly braided. She clutched the goat against her chest, just as Megha clutched her baby. And she was crying over the struggling goat as if it were her most precious possession. Two young boys were crying with her. The village women clustered around them, chattering about the escape of the unruly goat.

The goat is that woman's future, and it survives. *Jumbled, jagged, jumpy shots of the village woman, the wriggling goat, the frenetic children, the woman, the goat... Theatrical musical exclamations, the images and the soundtrack combining to capture the confusion and chaos.*

Manvi emerged from the wreck, staggering and bleeding. Manvi's past had been built on an illusion. The bedrock of her identity stemmed from a fantasy about love. She was the Woman Who Could Cast a Man Out of the City. Now, when Girish avoided her, the foundation of her confidence would be washed away. *Images of her tears, streaks of blood, disarrayed hair, wild eyes. The music louder and more dramatic, the soundtrack going into overdrive.*

Anu noticed the frown on Pranab's face as he helped Manvi cross the road and sit down with the women at the well. Pranab looked at Anu and waved reassuringly to indicate that Manvi was not badly hurt, and she felt the solid wall of his concern reach out to her.

As she walked across to help him, the TV serial in Anu's imagination faded. The cameras ceased their melodramatic close-ups of the four women, the sensational music died out. This episode of the serial was over.

Read more from HarperCollins India

Nothing is Blue
Biman Nath

It is the seventh century. The last of the ancient emperors rules over the Indian subcontinent. All is not well in his empire though, and there are palpable signs of unrest. Even the serene atmosphere at the Nalanda monastery – the biggest in the ancient world – is shaken by the political turmoil. It is also a time shrouded in secrets and mysteries. Some Buddhist monks have begun to dabble in tantric rituals. Elsewhere, a crucial astronomical discovery has been hushed up. A student monk from the monastery stumbles on these unpalatable secrets, and his life changes forever. It is a story that Xuanzang, the Chinese pilgrim visiting Nalanda, cannot afford to record. But it will haunt him endlessly.

A vivid recreation of the medieval India, *Nothing is Blue* is a tale of the cul-de-sacs of history, of pain and memory, hope and fate.

Silverfish
Saikat Majumdar

A retired schoolteacher in present-day Calcutta is caught up in
the labyrinth of rusty bureaucracy and political crime under a
communist government. Across a vast ocean of time, a widow
leads a life of stark suffering in a wealthy feudal household in 19th
century, British-ruled Bengal, at a time when widow burning has
gone out of practice but widow remarriage is far from coming into
vogue.

As their stories begin to connect, they weave a larger narrative
of historical forgetting, of voices that have been pushed out of the
nation's memory. And what we are left with is the intriguing tale
of two cities: the same geographical space separated by decades of
experience and neglect.

Without Dreams
Shahbano Bilgrami

Nineteen years after his father's murder, Haroon Rizwan returns
to the country of his birth to revisit his family home. Haunted
alternately by nightmare-visions of his father's death and the
frustrating inability to remember exactly what happened, Haroon
decides to search deeper within himself for answers. The visions
take him back to that fateful year, 1983, and to Abdul, the Rizwans'
servant boy. As Haroon relives his childhood – one troubled by his
father's abusive behaviour towards his mother – he comes to realize
that Abdul's past, with its undertones of violence, counterpoints his
own.

Without Dreams is the story of two boys growing up in a household
beset by violence in a country sharply divided along ethnic and class
lines. Like estranged brothers, Haroon and Abdul travel towards a
common destiny, till a terrifying moment changes their lives for ever.

Cappuccino Dusk
Kankana Basu

A wacky poetry-spouting boy, Mustafa, walks into the house of the argumentative Banerjees and turns life upside down for the four eccentric siblings – Som, Bonny, Sid and Mishti – and their absent-minded mother, Ira. Soon they're joined by a bumbling Shaivite cousin, a conservative Brahmin grandmother, a shy nature-loving cartoonist, a bubbly journalist, and a lonely neighbour. Coffee, conversation and laughter flow until circumstances force their lives into unexpected directions. Now, unlikely alliances must be forged and dangerous desires awakened as the Banerjees and their friends leave behind familiar warmth to explore uncharted territories.

Cappuccino Dusk is a tale of love, laughter, hopes and tragedies as its delightful menagerie of characters face life and its challenges head-on. Woven with wit and warmth, this first novel set in Mumbai takes us on a journey that both amuses and moves.

Damage
Amrita Kumar

When Gudda marries a Hindu, her mother Beatrice, a Christian
missionary, disinherits her and wills her house to Gudda's sisters.
Shortly after, a new government comes to power in New Delhi and
Christians are brutally attacked all over India. Gudda, her marriage
crumbling by then and with nowhere to go, returns to take care of
her mother, now ill and alone in the house. Even as mother and
daughter find ways to communicate after years of silence, Gudda's
sisters accuse her of trying to usurp the family property. In the midst
of chaos Gudda embarks on a journey to the Rajasthan desert,
to retrace the route of an ancient warrior race in whose past her
own origins lie. At a time when dilemmas of religious and cultural
identity are becoming the heart of conversations all over the world,
Damage is a searing comment on what matters to the individual in
the end, and what doesn't.

Rupture
Sampurna Chattarji

In the course of twenty-four hours, nine characters across five cities
are faced with a pressing need to examine their past. As each of
them confronts the realities within, the world itself explodes into
chaos, the disintegration of civic order mirroring the breakdown of
individual sanities.

A powerful first novel from a critically acclaimed poet, translator
and fiction-writer, *Rupture* is a book in which every word, every
emotion resonates with a heightened sense of intensity. Sampurna
Chattarji brings to her writing a poetry and potency that is rare, and
the sheer pace of the narrative pulls the reader in with its urgency.